"Everyone's Captive In One Way Or Another."

"Are you?" Had he moved closer? His male scent—expensive wool and subtle musk—tickled her senses.

"Absolutely." His voice was a low growl that took her by surprise, but not as much as the way he stepped in, lifted her chin deftly with his fingers and pressed his lips softly to hers.

This man is a beast. He chews people up and spits them out. He just confessed as much!

His low moan in her ear made her desire surge.

Was there magic in this place? If so, it might be the dark and scary kind. She certainly didn't feel fully in control of this situation—or even herself—at this moment.

And there was that family curse to contend with….

His kiss was alternately fierce and tender, drawing her in and taking her breath away. She'd never been kissed like this.

But he's your enemy.

D0595912

Dear Reader,

In this book, I was able to give free reign to my passion for castles by creating one for my characters. In the British Isles most castles have been destroyed in one conflict or another, and their ruins dominate the landscape around them with an air of romance and drama. A few medieval castles have resisted the attacks of successive marauders and stand as mighty as when they were built, including Edinburgh and Stirling castles in Scotland.

For this book I had fun imagining an even more ancient castle, with parts dating back to when the Romans attempted—unsuccessfully—to occupy Scotland. My imaginary castle is the seat of the ancient Drummond family, and their impressive legacy has become something of a burden to the man who inherits it. It takes a woman from far away to shake him out of his ordered existence and make him see his majestic home with fresh eyes. I hope you enjoy James and Fiona's story.

Best wishes,

Jennifer Lewis

JENNIFER LEWIS

A TRAP SO TENDER

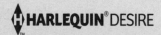 HARLEQUIN® DESIRE

Recycling programs for this product may not exist in your area.

ISBN-13: 978-0-373-73233-3

A TRAP SO TENDER

Printed in U.S.A.

www.Harlequin.com

Books by Jennifer Lewis

Harlequin Desire

†*The Prince's Pregnant Bride* #2082
†*At His Majesty's Convenience* #2094
†*Claiming His Royal Heir* #2105
Behind Boardroom Doors #2144
**The Cinderella Act* #2170
***The Deeper the Passion...* #2202
***A Trap So Tender* #2220

Silhouette Desire

The Boss's Demand #1812
Seduced for the Inheritance #1830
Black Sheep Billionaire #1847
Prince of Midtown #1891
**Millionaire's Secret Seduction* #1925
**In the Argentine's Bed* #1931
**The Heir's Scandalous Affair* #1938
The Maverick's Virgin Mistress #1977
The Desert Prince #1993
Bachelor's Bought Bride #2012

*The Hardcastle Progeny
†Royal Rebels
**The Drummond Vow

Other titles by this author available in ebook format.

JENNIFER LEWIS

has been dreaming up stories for as long as she can remember and is thrilled to be able to share them with readers. She has lived on both sides of the Atlantic and worked in media and the arts before she grew bold enough to put pen to paper. She would love to hear from readers at jen@jenlewis.com. Visit her website at www.jenlewis.com.

For Mia

One

Her enemy was handsome. Slate-gray eyes, dark hair and aristocratic features—every inch the Scottish laird.

She shook his offered hand. "Nice to meet you. I'm Fiona Lam."

"James Drummond."

I know. She smiled sweetly. His handshake was firm and his skin cool to the touch. Her own hand suddenly felt hot and she struggled not to pull it back. The glitzy cocktail party hosted by an international bank hummed around them, bright young things in expensive suits meeting and greeting each other, but somehow they all faded into the background. "I'm new to Singapore. Just moved here from San Diego."

"Really?" One elegant eyebrow raised.

"I sold my first business and I'm looking around for new opportunities. Do you work here?"

"Sometimes." He still held her hand. Cheeky devil.

No wonder he had a reputation as a ladies' man. "I have a place in Scotland."

The grand estate she'd heard about. She didn't care about that. She did want her hand back, though. It was getting hotter, and an unpleasant tingling sensation had started to trickle up her arm. She gave a firm tug and he released her fingers with the ghost of a smile.

She tried not to shake out her hand. "I've heard Scotland's beautiful."

"If you like mist and heather." His steely gaze was totally unblinking. No wonder he intimidated his business rivals.

"You don't?"

"I inherited them. Don't really need to have an opinion. Can I get you a drink?"

"Champagne." She sagged with relief as he turned to find a waiter. This guy was pretty intense. Which was fine. She didn't have to like him.

She just needed him to like her.

He returned with two bubbling glasses and handed her one. No one had warned her he was so good-looking. It was more than a little disconcerting. In her experience venture capitalists were usually men in their sixties with hair growing out of their ears. She sipped, then tried not to sneeze as the bubbles tickled the back of her throat. She wasn't a big fan of booze, but she wanted to look as if she fit into James Drummond's rarefied world.

He raised his sculpted chin. "What brings you to Singapore?"

"I'm looking into a couple of business opportunities."

Again, his brow lifted. "I'm in business myself. What do you do?"

"I just sold a company that makes decals. Smileworks." The name usually made people smile. It made her smile and she was still sad to have sold it. But not sad about all the money she'd made on the deal.

"I read about the buyout. Congratulations. That was quite a coup."

The sparkle of interest in his eyes had intensified. She felt a tiny rush of power—or was it pleasure? "Thanks. It was fun building Smileworks but I'd taken it as far as I could."

"So what's next for you?" He leaned forward, clearly intrigued.

She shrugged, annoyed to notice that her nipples had tightened beneath her black cocktail dress and hoping he wouldn't notice. "Not sure yet. I'll have to see what sparks my imagination."

In his dark gray suit and dark gray tie, James Drummond was sparking her imagination in all kinds of undesirable directions. He was so buttoned down that the prospect of tearing off his crisp white shirt or running fevered fingers through his carefully combed hair seemed an intriguing challenge.

Was it wise to bed an enemy? Probably not, but a little flirtation couldn't hurt. She needed to gain his trust, then figure out how to buy—or steal—her father's factory back.

She managed another sip of the unfamiliar champagne. She had to stay focused. Her dad needed her and at last she could prove to him she cared. It wasn't her fault she'd grown up nine thousand miles away, calling another man Daddy. She hadn't planned the first two decades of her life but she was in charge of the rest and she intended to right some of the wrongs that had been committed against Walter Chen. Starting with the wrongs committed by one James Drummond.

* * *

They left the cocktail party together, and James's driver took them to Rain, the hottest new restaurant, where even he had to pull strings to get a reservation.

"This place is stunning. I had no idea Singapore had so much nightlife." She stared around at the minimalist decor with its cool green lighting. "Clearly, I need to get out more."

"Got to keep the worker bees happy or we'd all fly off somewhere else."

He sat opposite her, pleased by the surprise of having dinner with a beautiful woman who'd been in his life for only one hour. Fiona had his attention. Her company, Smileworks, had created an international splash with its funky graphics and new concepts for things to stick decals to—like walls. That she'd already sold it and banked more money than most people made in a lifetime was impressive.

And she was beautiful as well as smart, with dramatic dark eyes framed by slightly arched brows, and a full mouth that begged to be kissed. Her American accent had surprised him, and added to the layers of intrigue. She was exactly the kind of woman he could see himself marrying.

And he needed to marry.

The waiter gave them shiny black menus. He watched her eyelashes flick lower as she scanned hers. Then she looked up and transfixed him with those bright eyes. "What do you recommend?"

"I've heard it's all good, but I can lend my personal recommendation to the sea urchin."

Her eyes widened. "I had no idea those were edible."

The waiter showed him a bottle of his favorite wine and he nodded. When the waiter had filled their glasses and left, he leaned in. "Last time I had the pigeon. That was good, too. All depends on whether you want to eat creatures of land, sea or air."

She laughed. "How about a pond?"

"The duck is very tender." He smiled and lifted his glass to her. "And I expect they could even make pond weed taste good if they wanted."

"A little salt and pepper, sauté it with garlic?" Humor sparkled in her lovely eyes. Then she raised her glass and took a sip. "That's some good wine."

A smile tugged at his mouth. "At four hundred dollars a bottle it should be. I like it."

"You spend more time in Singapore than Scotland?" She unfurled her napkin as she asked.

"I do. Scotland's not exactly an international business hub." Funny how she hadn't even asked him what he did yet. That was refreshing. Being new to Singapore, she obviously had no idea of his reputation, which was also a plus. It got tiresome explaining to people that you weren't a vulture, or—lately—that vultures played an important role in the circle of life. "You can work from anywhere these days. I do most of my work over the internet."

"I do, too, but nothing beats meeting people face-to-face." Fiona's face was lovely. Smooth skin with a radiant glow that contrasted with thick dark hair that swept to her shoulders. He wanted to run his fingers through that hair.

And if all went according to his current plan, he would.

"It's funny that you have a Scottish first name, when there's nothing Scottish about you."

She lifted her slim brow with a slightly defiant air.

"I do like plaid. I even bought a pair of plaid shoes the other day. What's Scottish about you?"

"Good question. I'm not sure anyone's ever asked it before. I'm probably the only person I've ever met who actually enjoys single malt whiskey."

She wrinkled her nose. "You're certainly the only one I've met. I tried it once and I won't be doing that again."

"I treat it with a healthy respect, myself, as it's killed a lot of my forebears."

"They were drinkers?"

"Drinkers, fighters, fast drivers, the type of men who go out looking for the end of a sword to run into."

Curiosity sparkled in her eyes, and stirred the arousal gathering low inside him. "And you're not like that?"

"I prefer to be holding the sword."

He expected a laugh, or at least a smile, but she simply seemed to consider his words for a moment. "I suppose that is a better position to be in. Are you afraid of ending up like your ancestors?"

"Can't say I am. Though I keep getting emails and letters from my American cousin who's decided it's her mission to save the Drummond family from an ancient curse by reuniting three parts of a lost chalice."

Her eyes widened. "A curse? Do you think there's anything to it?"

"I don't believe in that kind of nonsense. Hard work and common sense are the cure for most so-called curses I've heard about."

"You did say your ancestors kept wading into trouble." She raised a slim brow. "Maybe there's something to the legend. Where is the chalice supposed to be?"

"According to my cousin's last rather breathless email, she's already found two pieces. One was in the family home where she resides in New York—she's a Drummond herself by marriage—and the other was found in the ocean off an island in Florida, where it sank in a pirate ship three hundred years ago. She thinks the third piece was brought back to Scotland by one of my ancestors."

"How intriguing." She leaned forward, giving him a tantalizing whiff of her soft floral scent. "Are you going to look for it?"

Her obvious excitement stirred a trickle of interest in the idea. He'd almost forgotten about Katherine Drummond and her pleas for him to join in the hunt. He'd been so busy lately he couldn't remember if he'd even responded. "I don't know. Do you think I should?"

"Absolutely." Her eyes shone. "It's so romantic."

Romantic was good. He was already entertaining romantic thoughts about Fiona, whose black cocktail dress wrapped her slim, athletic figure like a glass around a shot of single malt. "She's convinced the third part of the cup is hidden somewhere on my Scottish estate. She's even offered a reward for the person who finds it. I've had to hire security to keep treasure hunters from digging up the lawns and climbing the battlements."

She laughed. "And you've never looked for it at all?"

"Nope. I know easier ways to earn a few thousand dollars."

"But it sounds like an adventure." Fiona glowed, and he found his own body temperature rising in response. He resisted the urge to loosen his collar, which suddenly felt tight. "I think you should search for it. Who knows what fabulous things might happen if you find the missing piece and put the chalice back together?"

"My life is pretty good right now."

"I bet there's at least one aspect of it that could be improved."

I do need a wife. He certainly wasn't going to tell her that. Singapore's conservative culture frowned on a man who was thirty-six years old and still playing the field. It was beginning to affect business. He'd been turned down by a potential partner in a very compelling project who let him know he didn't approve of his lifestyle.

Lifestyle? Just because he liked to mind his own business and control his own destiny didn't make him a womanizer. On the other hand, even serial monogamy began to look a bit flaky after nearly twenty years of dating, simply because of the sheer number of women involved.

There was no shortage of women ready, willing and able to marry him. They usually threw themselves at him once they got wind of the Scottish estate or the millions in investments. What he needed was a cool-headed and congenial business partner. Someone he could trust in the kind of legally binding contractual situation that modern marriage really was.

Someone—perhaps—like Fiona Lam.

She licked a droplet of champagne from her upper lip, sending a surge of heat crashing through him. Breathing deep, he shrugged out of his jacket. Fiona was a very attractive woman, and her high intelligence was even more of a turn-on than her lush lips or shapely legs.

"Or maybe I'm wrong?" She leaned back in her chair, eyes appraising him coolly. "Is there anything you want that you don't already have?"

He laughed. "Always. That's what gets me out of bed in the morning."

"The thrill of the chase?"

"Makes my venture capitalist heart pump hard."

"Maybe you're not so different from your Scottish ancestors. You're just excited by different quarry."

"You could be onto something. They wanted a stag, or the neighbor's estate, I want a nice international conglomerate with growth potential."

She smiled. "You're funny."

"I'm not so sure about that, but I am pretty predictable."

She tilted her head, sending a fall of shiny black hair to one shoulder. "Why haven't you ever married?"

He stilled. "How do you know I haven't?" Did she know more about him than she was letting on?

"No ring. And no tan line where the old ring used to be."

He relaxed slightly. Being somewhat notorious, he tended to be on guard when meeting new people. Besides, anyone reading a business magazine could know the basic facts of his life. It was hardly top-secret information. "Never met the right woman."

"Too picky?"

"Something like that. A marriage isn't like an investment, where it's worth taking a chance on because you can always get out."

"You can always get out, for the right price." A smile tilted her soft mouth.

He grimaced. "Usually the highest price the market will bear. Not attractive to a careful investor."

"You're too cautious to get married, aren't you?"

He nodded. "Or maybe it's just the family curse."

She laughed aloud, a pretty ringing sound, like the bells they used to play in the church back on the estate when he was a kid.

Where did that thought come from?

"I think you need to find the last part of that chalice and put it back together. Think of it as a hunt." She leaned forward, rested her elbows on the table and her neat chin on her interlocked fingers. "It'll be a great story to tell."

A crazy idea flashed into his brain. "Come look for it."

"What?" Her eyes widened.

"Come to Scotland. I have to take a trip back myself right now to deal with some estate matters. You said you'd like to visit. Take a break from the rat race and breathe some highland air."

She was silent, and he could almost hear the cogs turning in her brain. Her eyes sparkled and he could see the idea intrigued her. "But I don't even know you."

"I'm pretty well-known around town. Ask people about me."

"What will they tell me?" She looked deadly serious.

"That I play by my own rules, but always stand by my word." He hesitated, knowing what else she would hear. "That I'm happiest when sinking my teeth into a new business." He deliberately avoided the part about his alleged Casanova ways.

Her eyes had narrowed slightly, and she appeared to be considering his proposal. His pulse ratcheted and he realized how much he wanted her to accept. Even the usually unwelcome prospect of returning to the grim and vast baronial castle and the manager's endless to-do list seemed less daunting with the prospect of the lovely Fiona in residence.

"Okay." She spoke quietly, but without hesitation.

"You'll come?" He couldn't believe it.

"I will." She sat back in her chair, expression still serious. "I've always wanted to go to Scotland, I love the idea of looking for an ancient relic, and I have nothing better to do right now. Why not?"

"Why not, indeed?" They discussed dates for a minute or two and he sent a text to his pilot while the waiter served their food. For the first time in as long as he could remember, his nerves crackled with excitement over something other than an intriguing business deal. "Done. We leave tomorrow."

"Great." Fiona's voice faltered slightly. This was moving so much faster than she expected. "Who knew I'd be eating sea urchin and going to Scotland all in the space of one week?"

What would her dad think about her leaving so soon after she'd arrived? The main purpose of her stay here was to build their relationship. After ten days they'd barely managed to relax enough to hold a conversation, and now she was taking off around the world with his sworn enemy?

She'd have to explain her plan. He'd understand and know she was only doing it for him. He'd be so happy when she figured out how to wrest his factory back from James Drummond's octopuslike embrace. This man needed to be stopped, and she wasn't afraid to do it.

"Will you stay there with me?" This thought occurred to her for the first time almost as she said it. He'd asked her to come to his house and look for the cup. While snooping around his ancestral home might be fun, she couldn't achieve her main goal unless he was there.

"Of course. I wouldn't invite a guest and then take off." He frowned. "Then again, I probably have done that, but I promise I won't this time. I need to put in some face time there. The natives get restless if the lord of the manor goes AWOL for too long."

"Is it really like that?"

He nodded. "I don't understand why they care what I do, but they seem to feel I should be there judging flower displays at the village fete and hosting banquets on obscure saints' days."

"Very medieval." There was something sexy about that. Which just proved how loopy she could be. He obviously hated it and ran off to Singapore all the time to avoid his feudal responsibilities. "Do you get to have people executed if they cross you?"

"I've never tried." A tiny smile tugged at his broad, seductive mouth. "I don't think anyone's ever ticked me off that badly."

I might. She let her own secret smile slip across her lips. "Are they putting pressure on you to find a lady of the manor?"

He laughed. "They wouldn't dare." Then his eyes darkened. "Though I'm sure they would if they didn't think it would make me run for the hills."

They certainly wouldn't be too enthused about her, a snarky American with her roots in Singapore. No doubt they'd prefer a delicate Scottish rose with red-gold hair and pink cheeks, who thought arranging flowers on the church altar was the ideal way to spend a weekend.

Not that James was bringing her there to romance her. In fact, she had no idea why he did want her to come. She frowned and looked at him. His eyes smiled slightly when she met them, sending a frisson of…what? Excitement, terror and hot lust coursing right through her.

Did he really want her to find the cup? Surely someone closer to home would be a better choice. Did he want to bed her?

Yes. The subtle gleam in his eye made no secret of that. Maybe he was a lothario. And maybe he'd be disappointed in his efforts to add her to his list of conquests.

She took a bite of her sea urchin, sitting almost forgotten on her plate, and was surprised to find it tender and delicious. James was very distracting. She'd better make sure she kept her mind on her task—getting her father's factory back. "This is good."

"I told you it would be. Now you know you can trust me."

She laughed, partly because he said it so innocently, as if he really believed it. If she didn't know of his reputation as a heartless corporate shark, she'd have taken him for a genuinely nice guy. He certainly seemed generous and enthusiastic. Luckily for her, his reputation preceded him. "I don't trust that easily. I do apparently have a taste for adventure, though. I'm excited about coming to Scotland."

"You'll win the reward if you find the cup."

"If I do, I'll donate it to charity. I'm not exactly hurting for money after the sale of Smileworks."

"What are you going to do next?"

That's for me to know and you to find out after I've done it. She shrugged. "Whatever takes my fancy. I'm in no rush." Maybe she could convince him to sell her the factory for a pittance. She wasn't sure why he'd bought it in the first place. "What's your latest project?"

"I'm becoming interested in real estate. Sooner or later this recession will end and people will want everything bigger and better and newer than ever."

"And you plan to be poised to take advantage of that."

He sipped his wine. That mouth was wasted on a businessman. He should have been a pouting rock star. "I try to be ready for anything."

Her father's factory was centrally located in an old business district that was ripe for redevelopment into a yuppie paradise. The building was from the 1950s and looked like a giant shoebox. Until six weeks ago it had employed eighteen people and provided her father with his only source of income. But James had engaged in some skullduggery with the local government and managed to buy it out from under her dad for a pittance in unpaid taxes. At least that was how she understood it. All the workers had been laid off, and her dad was now facing bankruptcy, so the clock was ticking.

When she was younger, her dad had owned a chain of restaurants, but that had apparently disappeared. They'd had so little contact with him after she moved to the States with her mom that she was surprised to find him so close to the edge, when family legend had pegged him as a high-rolling, self-made tycoon.

She'd always planned to show him just how like him she was when she made her first million. Her anticipated triumph had been utterly destroyed by his sudden ruin. Now it looked as if she'd come to Singapore to crow over the father who abandoned her, when that was the very opposite of her intention.

Her heart squeezed. She'd grown up without her dad and she wasn't going to lose him now. "I try to be ready for anything, too. And I had no idea I was so ready to go to Scotland with a complete stranger."

He lifted his glass. "Here's to the unexpected."

She smiled and clinked hers against it. *If you only knew.*

Two

"These berms mark the edge of the estate." James nodded to the window of the fast-moving Land Rover that had picked them up at Aberdeen airport.

Fiona peered out. Anticipation coursed through her body. Which was ridiculous. She was here on the most underhanded mission, yet she felt excited as if she genuinely hoped to find that damn cup and maybe even have a torrid affair with James while she did it. Deep ditches on the side of the road swooped up into high walls of grass and trees. They drove straight along this avenue for almost twenty minutes. "How big is the estate?"

"Big. But don't worry. We'll reach the business end soon." Eventually, the road swung around and took them through a tall stone gateway. Hills soared around them, making her feel tiny in the dramatic landscape. "My ancestors liked privacy."

"And you don't?"

"Not that much." He smiled. "A wall between me and my neighbors is quite enough. I don't need a few miles."

"Then it's lucky you'll have me here to bother you."

"It is."

Her skin tingled at the affirmation that he was glad of her company. She should feel guilty that she was here only to get her father's factory back. She didn't, though. The reports she'd read of James's business practices had made her toes curl. He was all about the bottom line and clearly didn't care whom he steamrolled over on the road to more greenbacks. And he hadn't brought her here just to find some old cup. She wasn't the worldliest person, but she'd been around the block to know he had some ulterior motive himself, even if it was just a highland fling.

The road was dead straight, carved right through the undulating landscape in what must have been an engineering feat to rival building the pyramids. High hedges loomed ahead, and once they passed those her jaw dropped as a menacing storybook castle rose in front of them.

A complex of buildings, mossy-gray stone in styles that looked medieval, Tudor, Victorian, even Roman, spread in all directions. "It's huge."

"It was more or less a town in its heyday. Everyone lived inside the defended area. Some still do—the estate manager and his staff."

"I can see how a person could get lonely here."

"You don't know the half of it. Makes Singapore seem very welcoming by comparison."

Fiona stared at him for a moment, feeling sudden affection for this man who felt more at home in a bustling, noisy Asian city than in the baronial halls of his ancestors. He seemed more human all the time.

Again, not a good thing.

"You must need a large staff to keep this place alive."

"Not really. I know the villagers think I should do more with it, but as long as someone keeps the roof solid and the windows sealed, it takes care of itself. Sheep keep the grass down. A stone fortress is very low maintenance compared to a modern house."

Someone must climb on a scaffold almost weekly to keep those monster hedges at the entrance manicured to perfection. Maybe he had no idea how much work it took to keep the place running. He probably didn't care. It was all pocket change to him.

The car pulled up in a gravel courtyard the size of a football field. Not a weed in sight. Two men in dark suits carrying walkie-talkies appeared from behind more manicured bushes, but stilled at the sight of the car.

"The hired security. I don't know what my cousin was thinking when she announced a reward for finding the cup."

"She knew it would get people interested. Obviously she was right." James climbed out of the car, and the driver opened her door and helped her out. She was starting to feel like a royal dignitary with all this VIP treatment. It might be hard to go back to ordinary life after this.

An older man emerged from the house and he and the driver carried their bags inside after a brief exchange with James. "Is he your butler?"

James nodded. "We call Angus the household manager. Sounds more modern, don't you think?"

"Oh, yes." There was nothing modern about any of this. Which piqued her curiosity to get more of a glimpse into James Drummond's rarefied life. With no bags to carry, she walked across the vast expanse of gravel feeling rather at a loss. Her cute stiletto heels kept tipping her this way and that, and James's bold stride almost left her behind by the time they reached a veritable cliff of stone steps.

He turned and extended his arm. She had no choice but to take it. She tried to ignore the trickle of sensation that crept up her arm and across her body. You'd think a full day of travel in close proximity to the man might have killed any spark of sexual attraction. Unfortunately, however, it had stoked it into a steady flame. Good thing she was ruled by her head and not more unpredictable parts of her anatomy.

The doorway into the house looked more suited to a grand cathedral. She almost expected the smell of incense and the murmur of monks; instead, she was greeted by an aroma of bacon and the distant barking of dogs.

"You have dogs?"

"Not me. I travel too much. The hounds for the local hunt are kept on the estate. They gather here to hunt and I join them when I'm around. I won't do it when you're here, of course."

"Why not?"

"It would be rude of me to leave you."

"Maybe I could come, too?" She lifted a brow.

He frowned. "Hunting is done on horseback."

She laughed, a loud, ringing sound that bounced off the stone walls. "I may be American but I'm not an idiot."

"You ride?"

"Of course." She decided to stride ahead, as if this news were nothing special. Inside she was glowing with triumph. James Drummond obviously had no idea what he had on his hands with her. "Where will I sleep?"

"Upstairs." He followed her. "I'll show you myself."

Her bedroom looked fit for a queen. Perhaps one about to be executed in the Bloody Tower. A high, four-poster bed stood in the center of the room, curtains pulled back halfway to reveal rich brocade bedding. Tiny leaded windows filled the room with a gloomy half light. The large Oriental rug was worn and faded, possibly by hundreds of years of use. What appeared to be a priceless Ming vase stood high on the stone mantel. "Your family doesn't go in for redecorating, do they?"

He chuckled. "Not since about 1760. You could say we're a bit set in our ways."

"At least you don't waste money on passing fads."

"Not often. These newfangled glass windows were controversial when they first came out, but we like them."

She smiled. "And you can still open them to pour boiling oil on marauders."

"Absolutely. The designers thought of everything."

"Is there a bathroom, or have those not established themselves in fashion for long enough?"

He gestured to a low wood door. She pulled the handle with some trepidation, and was surprised when it opened into a large, heavily marbled room with an appropriately antique-looking tub and sink and toilet in sparkling condition. At least she wouldn't have to wash herself from a jug.

"There's no shower, I'm afraid. We're still not convinced those are here to stay, but water does come out of the taps, so you won't have to call for Angus to bring it."

"That is a relief. I'm not sure I want Angus seeing me in a towel." She wanted to laugh, but somehow managed not to. "I am beginning to worry about finding this cup."

"Why?" He frowned, which annoyingly made him look even more handsome.

"The place makes big look small."

"It's sprawling, but quite simple to navigate, and there's little clutter to deal with. The Drummonds always seem to have gone in for a sparse, minimalist style."

"How forward thinking."

"Are you tired?"

"No. I was thinking about that bacon and what lucky person might get to eat it."

He laughed. "Let's go."

Breakfast was served in a grand hall. They sat at a long wooden table, its surface polished to a high sheen. The blue-and-white porcelain plates had probably been imported from China in the 1700s. After they ate their fill from a collection of covered dishes, James offered to give her a whirlwind tour of the castle.

"You might be the first non-Drummond to see inside the east wing this century," he murmured, as he pulled open a wood door studded with dark iron. He ducked through the low entranceway.

"Are you sure you won't have to kill me because I've seen too much?" Her skin prickled with excitement, partly from gaining entry to the Drummonds' inner sanctum, but mostly from continued proximity to James.

"Time will tell." He shot her a dark gray glance that made her freeze for a second, until she saw the humor sparkling behind his steely visage.

She swallowed. Time would tell all, but she'd make sure to put plenty of distance between them before that happened.

He gestured for her to enter. The hallway was narrow and she brushed against his arm as she passed. Even through his expensive shirt, his touch still sent a hot flash of awareness coursing through her. What did his body look like under his elegant armor? Was he muscled and athletic, or was that just her fevered imagination at work?

Her heart pumped faster as she entered the low hallway with its coffered ceiling. Her cute shoes clacked annoyingly on the flagstone floor. James could probably lock her up in one of these rooms and it would be months—years—before anyone found her. "Where are you taking me?"

"The oldest part of the house. It's where Drummonds piled their junk once they cleared it out of the more inhabited rooms. It's the first place I'd suggest looking for the cup piece."

"What kind of shape is it?" Online research into the story had told her it was the base of the cup they were looking for, but no need for him to know she'd done some digging on her own.

"Round, I'd guess. It's the part that sits on the table, the base, so it could be a hexagon or similar."

"I hope it hasn't been thrown away over the years."

"Or melted down to make bullets. That's the kind of thing the Drummonds might do with miscellaneous metal."

"They sound a lovely bunch, your ancestors."

"'Keep thy blade sharp' is the family motto. It's right on the crest under the raven's claws."

That might explain James's ruthless pursuit of his goals. He had no idea she even knew of his reputation. She decided to call his bluff. "You seem so different."

"Am I?" He didn't look at her, but out a small leaded window, at the white sky. "Sometimes I wonder."

"Why do you think of yourself as ruthless?" Maybe she could make him peer into his own hard heart and appeal to his sense of right and wrong to get her father's factory back. Then he'd be grateful to her for helping him see the light. They could be friends—or lovers?—and live happily ever after.

Reality smacked her in the face as his laugh bounced off the thick stone walls. "I think I'm the last person you should ask about that."

She decided not to push further. Not yet. She was here as his guest, and she didn't want him getting suspicious about her motives. The hallway seemed to go on forever, and all the doors along it were closed. "What's behind all these doors?"

"Small bedrooms. Probably once inhabited by vassals."

"What the heck is a vassal?"

He chuckled. "Hangers-on. People who lived off the good grace—what little there was of it—of the auld Drummonds."

Like me. "Interesting. What would they get out of keeping such people around?"

"People who are obligated come in useful when you need a favor. Or some dirty work done."

She glanced behind her, for no good reason. Had James brought her here for reasons of his own? She thought she was so cunning to get invited into the heart of his empire, but maybe he had his own nefarious plans for her.

The fearsome clack of her own shoe heels was getting on her rather raw nerves.

Suddenly James took a turn to the left and pulled back an iron bolt on a tall wood door. "Welcome to the oldest part of the castle."

The door opened onto a sort of balcony. She stepped through it and peered over a stone rampart into a square-shaped hall. Antique wood furniture sprawled uninvitingly on the flagstone floor of the hall about thirty feet below where they stood. Above them a ceiling of great wood beams had probably held up the roof for a thousand years.

James marched along a gallery and down a flight of narrow wood stairs toward the main floor. She followed slowly, staring around the space. She could almost feel the presence of all the men and women who must have breathed the air in this space over the years. "This is incredible. How come you don't use it?"

"The newer parts of the castle are more comfortable. And they have heat."

A grand stone fireplace stood cold and empty. Visions of a roaring flame, and maybe something roasting on a spit, crowded her mind. "How strange to think that your ancestors have lived here since the day it was built."

"They haven't." He stared up at a carved crest above the fireplace. "Gaylord Drummond lost the whole estate in a game of dice in the eighteenth century. That's how some of the Drummonds ended up in America. He gambled and drank away everything they owned except the one mysterious cup everyone's so excited about, so his three sons took off for the untamed shores of the New World to make their fortunes. There they apparently split up the cup and each took a piece, vowing to reunite it one day." His stony gaze still rested on the chiseled stone.

"And one of them ended up back here."

"He made a killing in beaver pelts up in Canada."

"Poor beavers."

"They used to make hats out of their fur. Very waterproof, apparently. He made his fortune, then sailed back here and bought the place from the son of the farmer who had won it from his father."

"And presumably he brought his piece of the cup with him."

James shrugged. "Can't say I care one way or the other."

"You're terrible. It's a part of your family history."

"I keep this pile going. That's my contribution to the family history. Maybe I should start playing dice. Losing it would save me a fortune."

"You don't mean that."

"Not really." He finally looked at her, and again his gray gaze stole her breath. "Though sometimes I wish I did."

She thought she saw emotion somewhere behind his stony facade. How could you not feel a powerful sense of history—even destiny—while standing in such an ancient and dramatic space? If she could feel it, she knew ancestral pride must beat somewhere in James Drummond's cold heart. She could hardly imagine being heir to such a kingdom even if, by today's standards, it was rather remote and unpopulated.

She drew in a long breath and stared about her. "I think it's magical."

His attention focused on her again, its icy blast like a laser. Did he suddenly suspect her of trying to worm her way into his affections so she could be mistress of this place? Women must have been trying for decades. She regretted her cheesy enthusiasm, and managed a casual shrug. "But I can see how a condo near Orchard Road would be easier to maintain."

He laughed. "Unquestionably." His eyes narrowed

and she felt herself under scrutiny again. For a split second his gaze seemed to scan her body like an unemotional piece of precision equipment, but somehow it left her nipples tingling, her belly quivering and her knees shaky.

She wheeled around. Maybe if she couldn't see him he'd have less power over her. It was infuriating how a simple glance from him sent her pulse racing. He was her enemy, for crying out loud. Perhaps he brought all his potential conquests here to astonish them with his family grandeur and made them swoon into his arms.

"So, where's the cup?" She walked farther away from him, trying to sound nonchalant.

"Your guess is as good as mine."

"Hardly. You know where the nooks and crannies are." There didn't even seem to be any that she could see. Though there were some battered wooden doors along one wall. "You know, the places where they locked up their enemies and left them for dead?"

"Oubliettes are more of a French thing. We Scots prefer to slit their throats in broad daylight then have a party."

She had to laugh. "A simple folk."

"Yes. Reporters have accused me of similar behavior in my business dealings." Humor glittered in his cool gaze.

She cursed the way her heart fluttered. He'd just admitted that he was a ruthless bastard! How could she still be attracted to him? She should be worried about her own sanity. "Do you think they're right?" She tried to maintain a steely stare.

"Maybe." He turned and strode across the room, leaving her standing there, heart pounding and unspoken words crowding her brain.

You stole my father's business and left him penniless and devastated. She had to keep a cool head until she figured out how to get it back. She couldn't let him know that she was on the side of those who despised him. "I guess that's just business, huh?"

He wheeled around, and she was surprised to see a half smile on his face. "It's a relief to talk to someone who understands."

She blinked. Okay. She'd opened this trapdoor and fallen in all by herself. "I haven't had to slit any throats yet."

He laughed. "You're still young."

"Not really." How arrogant of him. He was only a few years older than she. "I have plenty of life experience."

Laughter danced in his eyes. "Of course you do."

She wanted to slap him. "I started my first business when I was twelve."

"A lemonade stand?"

"Buying old computers and reselling them for scrap." She lifted her chin. "Much more profitable than squeezing lemons." No need to mention she'd had the lemonade stand, too.

He moved closer to her. Which was unsettling considering that they had about an acre of space around them. "I started my first business at eleven."

"Competitive, aren't you?" She raised a brow. All the tiny hairs on her body stood on end, prickling with awareness as he moved even closer.

"Very. Some have even said it will be my downfall."

Maybe sooner than you think. "What was your first business?"

"I bought wholesale chocolate bars and resold them to the desperate souls at my boarding school."

"A captive audience."

"The best kind." His shoulders were broad, almost straining against the elegant cut of his shirt. The great room was cool, but she could feel her body temperature spiking as he shifted his stance. His gray gaze rested right on her face, thoughtful, daring her to argue with him.

She straightened her own shoulders and raised herself to her full height, which unfortunately was a good half a foot less than his. "Is it hard to find a captive audience these days?"

"Not at all." He held her gaze for a heartbeat. "Everyone's captive in one way or another."

"Are you?" Had he moved closer? She didn't see him move his feet, but he was now so near she could lift her hand and touch him. His male scent—expensive wool and subtle musk—tickled her senses. Her nipples now strained against her bra, and she hoped he didn't notice.

"Absolutely." His voice was a low growl that took her by surprise, but not as much as the way he stepped in, lifted her chin deftly with his fingers and pressed his lips softly to hers.

Electric voltage zapped through her. Her body temperature shot skyward as his tongue touched hers. *I'm kissing James Drummond.*

She felt the weight of his palms settle on her lower back. Her breath now came in unsteady gasps, and her hands crept up to his torso and fisted themselves in his shirt.

This man is a beast. He chews people up and spits them out. He just confessed as much!

His low moan in her ear made her desire surge. Her fingers dug into his hard back. His rough skin created pleasurable friction against her cheek as he shifted the angle of the kiss and plunged deeper, making her arch her back and lean into his arms.

Uh-oh. Instead of fighting him off, she gripped him tighter and kissed him back with all the strength she possessed.

His scent was intoxicating. Surprisingly masculine and rugged, betraying the man hidden beneath the expensive designer clothes. She could feel the raw passion of his warlike ancestors surging through them both.

Was there magic in this place? If so, it might be the dark and scary kind. She certainly didn't feel fully in control of this situation—or even herself—at this moment.

And there was that family curse to contend with....

James's strong hand squeezed her buttock, which made her squirm. Her breasts bumped against his chest, and his other hand rose to skim her nipple with his thumb. His lips never left hers. His kiss was alternately fierce and tender, drawing her in and taking her breath away. She'd never been kissed like this.

He's your enemy.

This is probably exactly what his ancestors did with their enemies. The female ones, at least. She was being ravished. Why did it feel so good?

Her fingers had somehow wandered into his thick hair. She pressed the length of her body against his, and the thickening of his arousal made her heart beat faster. James Drummond seemed so cool, so controlled, that it only heightened her desire to feel him surging within her with heat and passion.

There was definitely more to this man than met the eye, or was written about in the columns of *Investor's Business Daily.* The way she felt right now, she could easily imagine peeling off his shirt and pants and making love to him right there on the cold stone floor of his ancestral castle.

But he pulled back. His hands slid from her waist and his lips slipped away from hers. An icy chill seemed to replace his touch. She opened her eyes—how long had they been closed?—and found herself blinking in the cold light of the empty hall.

James's eyes were narrowed, his face hard. "I hadn't intended for that to happen." He shoved a hand through his tousled hair. "Yet."

Three

Fiona smoothed the front of her black shirtdress. She hadn't changed since getting off the plane so it was probably rumpled even before James started roaming his hands over it. She couldn't believe she'd let him smooch her before she'd been here one entire day.

The word *yet* said it all. She now knew he'd fully intended to enjoy her in his bed, but after a suitable preamble of flirtation. Apparently, he'd grown impatient, and she'd fallen right into his arms like the fawning girls who no doubt cooed over him on every continent.

"I didn't intend for that to happen at all." She tried to look calm. "In fact, I'm still not sure what did happen."

"I think they call it kissing." His narrowed gaze showed only the coldest glint of humor. "And it's entirely too early in the day for it, apart from any other objections."

Her body still pulsed with arousal. Her fingertips

itched to touch his hard body, and her lips ached for the crush of his mouth. Who was he to suddenly announce it was a big mistake? "You started it."

Her childish retort hung in the air for a moment and she wished she could take it back. It was true, though.

His eyes widened very slightly. "I didn't notice you fighting me off."

"Maybe I was just trying to be a polite guest." This was getting sillier every moment.

One side of his arrogant mouth tilted in a wry smile. "Your manners are impeccable."

Irritation surged inside her, mingling with the almost painful desire that had sensitized her whole body. She raised herself to her full, not very impressive height. "I don't know about yours."

He raised a brow. "I have to agree with you." Then he frowned. "I'm not sure whether an apology is in order or whether that would be downright rude under the circumstances."

She drew in a shaky breath. "Maybe we should just act like it didn't happen."

"I don't think so." His gaze drifted lower. Not to anywhere obvious, like her breasts, but to her collarbone, which felt singed by his hot, dark gaze, then to her hands, which were now knotted in front of her.

"I'm not good at pretending."

He laughed. "Me, either. Okay, it happened and damn it, I enjoyed it."

She fought a smile that wanted to rip across her mouth. "No comment." Her enjoyment was so obvious there was no need to encourage him to gloat with triumph. "So, the cup. Where were we?"

James glanced around the room, as if wondering

where exactly they were. "I confess I'm not entirely sure. Certainly not where I thought we would be."

She laughed. Couldn't help it. It was probably all the tension—sexual and otherwise—that had built in the air around them. "Let's keep moving forward, shall we? And try to stay focused this time?"

"I like a woman with a good head on her shoulders."

"I can tell." She lifted her chin. "What's through that door?" She marched forward, determined to have some say in where this was going. Drifting along, allowing James to lead the way, was obviously dangerous.

"Try the handle."

She reached out, wondering what could be the worst-possible scenario for what they'd encounter on the other side. "What if it's a closet full of your family skeletons?"

"If one of them is clutching a cup, we're well on our way."

"If the Drummonds in New York found the stem, and the ones in Florida found the part you drink from, there isn't much cup for skeletal fingers to wrap around."

"Are you afraid to open that door?"

"Not at all." Her hand still clutched the small round handle, and she forced herself to turn it. With her luck it would be locked anyway. It swung open suddenly, almost pulling her into the room with it. She let go of the handle as if it burned. The room was piled high with furniture. Literally, it was piled almost to the rather low ceiling. Chairs and tables and chests, all obviously old and made of unpainted dark wood. "I think we found the junk room."

"Interesting." James stepped past her and into the room. "I've never been in here. I don't think I ever even noticed the door before." He looked around at the stacks of furniture that blocked their entrance. "You certainly are bringing something to this quest."

"Let's hope it's good luck that I'm bringing."

"I'm not at all sure, but I'll take my chances." His challenging gray gaze met hers.

Her heart kicked violently in response. Partly because a simple glance from him had that effect on her, and partly because she hadn't come here to bring him good luck.

"I bet some of these pieces are quite valuable."

"Do you know anything about antique furniture?" He rubbed at the finish of a nearby upside-down chair.

"Nothing at all."

"Me neither. I guess we'll just leave it here for the next generation to rediscover. Though I suppose we should check all the drawers for cup bottoms." He tugged on the brass handle of an elaborately carved chest. The drawer didn't budge.

"Let me try." She needed something to do. Her nerves were all on edge. She grabbed the handle and tugged on it. It came off in her hand, revealing sharp brass nails. "Oh."

"Looks like we'll have to keep you away from the priceless artifacts." His eyes sparkled with amusement.

"I'm sure it will be easy to fix." She looked at the handle in her hand. The nails made it look like a weapon. "Though maybe we should leave that to a professional." What little she did know about furniture told her that this little carved chest was several hundred years old.

James wrapped his long, strong fingers around the outside of the drawer and pulled it out as if it were a matchbox. Empty.

"That was an anticlimax." She heaved a sigh of relief, then wondered why. Was she worried they'd find this dumb cup base too soon and she'd have no excuse to stay here?

He pulled out the next drawer. Also empty, and very stained with something that looked like black ink. "Is that the blood of your ancestors' enemies, perhaps?"

"Nope. Too dark. There's a bloodstained floorboard in one of the upstairs bedrooms that resists all attempts to clean it. It's where one of my forebears was murdered by his manservant."

"Yikes. I guess that's the family curse in action."

"No doubt. It's quite a different color than this, though. Much richer. Almost like a wood stain."

"I'll have to remember that if I need to refinish something cheaply." She blew out another breath as he closed the drawer. She turned and lifted the lid on a nearby piece built like an old steamer trunk, but made of blackened oak carved with oak leaves. The lid opened easily, and the contents made her gasp. "This entire chest is filled with cup bases!"

James moved over to where she stood blinking at all the wide bases with their narrow stems. He let out a loud laugh. "Those are candlesticks."

"Oh. Of course they are." She cursed her stupidity. "I suppose that's a perfect example of seeing things the way you want them to be."

He picked one up and twisted it in the light. Like the others, it was a dark metal, tarnished to a dull, sheenless finish. "I guess these all went out of style overnight when they wired the place for electricity. Not that this wing ever got wired. I suppose they just shoved them all here out of the way."

"Funny to think how important these once were."

"They still are. We lose power quite often here." He

smiled at her, which made her stomach do an alarming shimmy. "Wait until we get a storm, you'll see."

She fought the urge to shiver. "I'd worry about all the ghosts coming out to party."

"I don't worry about them." He shoved his hand into the tangle of candlesticks.

"So there are ghosts?"

"I'd imagine so." He plucked one out and turned it in the light. "But as long as they leave me alone I won't bother them, either."

She stared. James Drummond was turning out to be quite different than she'd imagined. "I guess we should go through these and see if any of them could be a cup base. They are more or less the same shape. How big is the cup?"

He frowned. "I don't know. I haven't seen pictures of it. I suppose I should call Cousin Katherine and get all the details now that we're officially on the prowl for it."

"I bet she'll be thrilled."

"She will. Let's ask her to send some photos of the other pieces."

Katherine was out. James left a message explaining their situation and asking her to call.

Exhausted from their long trip, they ate an early dinner of beautifully prepared mini hens with some sort of fruity sauce and went to their separate rooms. She locked the door from the inside with the great iron key in the lock.

Not that James was likely to come looking for her after midnight, of course, but after what happened that afternoon...

She woke up in the dead of night with no idea what time it was. She'd fallen asleep like someone plunging into a coma and hadn't taken the time to keep her phone handy. The sky must have been overcast, as there was no hint of a moon. The room was a black hole.

With ghosts probably hanging around in the corners, watching her.

She pulled the covers up over her shoulders. That kiss had been crazy. It came out of nowhere and blew her off her feet like a Santa Ana wind. She had no idea he was that attracted to her. She'd been ogling him, sure, but she was pretty confident she had her lust under control. She wasn't usually given to bouts of groping and fondling strange men she'd just met.

He must have been feeling the same way. She shifted into the mattress with a swell of satisfaction. So, James Drummond thought she was hot.

Then she bit her lip. She was here to help her father. James Drummond's baser instincts were interesting to her only in so far as they'd help her get that factory back.

She sat up. There had been times when she'd almost forgotten about her father and that accursed factory, but now that she was away from Drummond's seductive gaze she should focus on what was really important.

Determined to find her phone, she slid her feet gingerly over the edge of the bed, hoping no spectral hands would grab at her ankles.

Stop being a wuss. The Persian rug felt threadbare under her toes, and a floorboard creaked alarmingly when she leaned her weight on one foot. Heart pounding, she crept across the room to the chair where she'd left her purse. Groping in the dark, she found her phone and let out a sigh of relief. She scurried back to the bed and climbed under the covers, then pulled up her father's number.

It rang the inevitable four times before he answered with a gruff, "Hello."

"Hi, Dad." She smiled at the sound of the words. She'd longed all her life to have a relationship with her father. She'd gone almost twelve years without even seeing him, and she was still angry with her mother for insisting that it was best to leave him alone.

"Who is it?" He did have an abrasive tone. She could see he wasn't a good match for her bubbly, artistic mother.

"It's Fiona." Who else could he think it was? He didn't have any other children. He was funny. "You won't believe where I'm calling from."

Suddenly she wondered if she should tell him. Would he believe she'd come all the way to Scotland just to help him out, or would he suspect she had entirely different motives in climbing into James Drummond's bed? Or one of them, at least.

"Where are you, Fifi?"

The term of endearment made her smile. If anyone else called her that she'd knock the person flat, but every conversation with her dad was a dream come true. "I'm in Scotland. At James Drummond's estate." She held her breath, waiting to see if he'd explode in a volley of abuse at the man he hated so much.

But dead silence hung in the air. She heard noise, like something happening at the other end of the line.

"I'm here to get your factory back, Dad."

"What? You can't do that. It's gone. That bastard stole it." His words burst into her ear, so loud she almost dropped the phone.

"He owns it, yes, but he hasn't done anything with it. As long as it's still standing, I can buy it back."

"He won't sell it."

This was true. She'd had a local real estate agent approach him and met with a firm refusal. But hopefully getting to know him would change things. "Every item has a price at which it becomes disposable." Even she had her price when they finally offered her so much money for Smileworks that she couldn't say no. "I'll convince him."

"He's an evil man."

"Not evil." She frowned. "Just misguided." Not unlike her father. Her mom had told her unflattering stories about him when she was growing up. Not all at once, but a little at a time. How he never uttered anything but criticism, worked twenty-three hours of the day and put every penny he earned back into the business so she had to make meals with rice and broth. Not the existence a young bride dreams of. Now that Fiona was an adult, she understood that everything worth achieving required a sacrifice. Her father and mother were just cut from different cloth: her mom's soft and flowery and her dad's crisp and tailored. She knew she was more like him. "He's not so bad, really."

"Why did he invite you? Is he trying to take advantage of you?"

Yes. At first she wasn't sure why he had invited her. Now she had a better idea. Strangely, it didn't scare her as much as it should. "Nothing like that. I'm supposedly here to help him look for a lost family artifact. We're searching through rooms of old junk."

"You be careful around that snake."

"Don't worry, I will." She'd have to put a double lock on her chastity belt. His hard, serious gaze had a disconcerting effect on her libido. "I'm trying to get to know him better so I can come up with a good plan. I'm currently leaning toward telling him I need to buy a building in Singapore as part of my next business. If he's as ruthless as they say, he won't mind selling as long as he's screwing me over."

"Don't give your money to that demon. He stole it from me."

"I know. Did you call the lawyer I told you about?" Surely if it was illegally obtained, her dad could get it back through the courts.

"Pah, lawyers. They'll just take more of my money and keep it."

"So he paid your taxes and got to keep the building? I don't really understand how that can happen."

"I was a little late with them. Not much, you understand. Just a little late."

How late? The government office she'd contacted said he'd lost the property through nonpayment but wouldn't reveal the details. Her dad firmly maintained that James had stolen it. Her relationship with her dad was still in a delicate, early stage and she didn't want to do anything that might embarrass him and drive him away. "I'll figure something out. Anyway, I wanted to let you know where I am so you don't worry."

"It sounds like I have good reason to worry, Fifi. You watch out for yourself with that *ang mo gui*."

"I will." She wanted to protest that James didn't have red hair, but of course the term *ang mo gui* was a generalized slang for Westerners that happened to mean "red-haired devil." "I can handle myself just fine." She glanced around the dark bedroom, reluctant to hang up the phone and lose her lifeline back to the real world. It was 3:00 a.m., with hours of darkness between now and morning. And who knew how many auld ghosts hung and hovered in the corners. "When I get back I want to take you to my new favorite restaurant." Hopefully to give him the good news that she'd regained control of his factory, but no sense getting overconfident.

"I'd love that, Fifi. It'll be my treat."

She swallowed. She wasn't sure he could even buy her dinner at McDonald's at the moment, but he'd be terribly upset if he knew she knew that. She had to come up with all kinds of creative stratagems to pay for their meals and buy him presents. His pride had no doubt played a part in his fall—a lesson she could learn from. "Great. You'd better not call me here, just in case. I don't want them to figure out I'm your daughter. I'm keeping everything secret."

He laughed, obviously delighted by the subterfuge. "My lips are sealed."

"I'll call again soon." She hung up, with a sudden rush of emotion and happiness that she had a second chance to grow close to her father. She wasn't going to blow it. He'd always wished for a son to carry on his name, but she'd show him that a daughter could be even better.

Her next encounter with James came at the breakfast table. Bored and restless alone in her room, she grew brave and ventured downstairs by herself. She hadn't fallen back to sleep after her conversation with her father, and now she was starving. Dishes of bacon, a rack of cold toast with butter and marmalade, a vat of jellified oatmeal. All very austere and aristocratic. She wolfed down some toast and bacon, and three cups of brutally strong tea, and was feeling fairly human by the time he strode in.

"Sorry I wasn't down first. I was more tired than I thought."

"No worries. I found my way here. I might get used to having breakfast waiting for me every morning."

"Would you like coffee? We do have some, way up in a cupboard somewhere."

"I'll survive on tea. I like to go native when I'm in a new place."

"Katherine emailed me pictures of the other two parts of the cup. I've just sent them to you."

She pulled out her phone and looked at hard-to-read images of dark metal against a white background. "She's very excited that I'm finally looking for it. I didn't have the heart to tell her that I'm using security guards to prevent people from combing the estate for it and claiming her reward."

Fiona smiled. "We'd better find it quick before she raises the reward to attract more people."

"Too true." James was more annoyingly handsome than ever. He wore loose riding breeches with tall leather boots and a checked shirt, which should have looked silly but made him seem tall and dashing and like the lord and master of all he surveyed. "I'm going riding this morning and I thought you might join me, if you're interested." His eyebrow lifted slightly. Was he calling her bluff? Maybe he didn't believe she could ride.

"I'd love to." She smiled coolly. "I hope it's not against the law to ride in jeans and loafers."

"We have so many old laws here I just assume everything's forbidden and go ahead with it anyway." He piled bacon, toast and some bright orange scrambled eggs onto a plate. "Luckily the place is so big and remote there's no one around to stop me."

"Good." Her pulse had quickened. Possibly from the prospect of galloping through the Scottish countryside, but more likely from the early-morning vision of James, with his dark hair wet and slicked back, and droplets of water still clinging to his neck and dampening the collar of his shirt. "Do you miss riding when you're in Singapore?" She still found it odd that he chose to spend most of his time there when he had his own grand empire here in Scotland.

"Not at all. I play polo at least twice a week." He drank some tea.

"Oh." Of course. No wonder he looked so fit and muscular.

"Do you play?"

"No. I've never tried it. I'd love to, though."

He raised a brow. "Really? We'll have to look into that when we're back in Singapore."

Her heart beat faster. Damn, she wished she could take him up on his offer. She'd always wanted to play polo but never had the chance. Going for trail rides and the occasional jumping competition was a pretty exclusive experience back in Cali, and she'd felt privileged to do that. But of course by the time they were back in Singapore, James would likely know who she really was and probably hate her guts, so she wouldn't be invited to his polo club.

If she was successful, at least. Regret unfurled in her heart. It was almost a shame that James had to be her enemy. She could have had a lot of fun with him.

After breakfast she changed into jeans and James led her to the stables, a long stone building with an elegant slate roof. Tall, magnificent horses peered out over freshly painted stable doors. "You have a lot of horses."

"Eight." He strode along the cobbled walk in front of the building. "That's more than enough work for Mick."

"Is he the groom?"

"The trainer. He rides them every other day. Toby is the head groom."

Even the stables were a small industry in this well-run machine of luxury and privilege. And he thought the place desolate and deserted!

"I think you should ride Taffy." He indicated a large gray horse with a kind eye.

"She looks lovely." Her halter and lead rope hung next to the door. "Should I bring her out, or is there a large staff for that?"

He laughed. "Bring her out. I always groom and tack up myself. It's the only way to know what mood they're in before you go out looking for trouble."

Taffy put her head right down into the halter and stood like a rock while she buckled it. She led her out and was surprised her hooves didn't clatter on the cobbles.

"Is she barefoot?" She glanced down and mentally answered her own question before he could answer.

"Yes. I keep all my horses unshod if they can handle it. Their feet adapt to handle their work and it's healthier for them. People stare and point but I get the last laugh when their horse loses a shoe in the middle of a hunt."

Fiona blinked. James was full of surprises. She wouldn't have thought someone like him would put a moment's thought into the well-being of his animals.

"You can tie her up here. I'll bring out the grooming kit." He pointed to a large iron ring, gleaming black, no doubt from the invisible work of skilled hands. She tied up the very polite Taffy, who outside her stall was absolutely enormous, and let her sniff her hand.

James returned with an elegant wooden grooming kit and a tall bay horse with steam pouring from its nostrils. "Poor Dougal has been cooped up in his stall for a month. He's a bit fresh."

Fiona stared. He was going to ride that thing? "He's very handsome. How do you choose your horses?"

"Gut instinct. I bought most of them as babies. An old school friend of mine is a breeder and he suckers me into visiting his stud at least once a year."

The horses were so clean someone had probably already groomed them that morning. She dusted Taffy off with a soft brush, and a young man appeared with two saddles and bridles. "Let me put that up there for you, ma'am." She let him heft the polished saddle onto Taffy. Probably a good thing since the mare's back was well above the top of Fiona's head. The mare put her head down so Fiona could slip the bridle on, then the groom brought over a polished wood mounting block the size and shape of a flight of six steps. In a flash of disappointment, she realized she had been hoping James would have to give her a leg up.

What's wrong with you, Fiona? Keep your mind on the reason you're here. James may have pretty horses and a fancy castle but he's a cold, cruel man who makes his millions by exploiting others.

She didn't entirely convince herself, but she managed to climb into the saddle and get her mind off the way James's well-cut breeches emphasized his muscled rear end.

Taffy seemed unphased by a new rider, and quietly followed James and his snorting steed out of the cobbled courtyard and down a lane past high stone walls. They passed through a high gateway and down a short hill through some woods. James kept asking if she was okay. He obviously thought that she'd fibbed about being able to ride and expected her to reveal her incompetence at any minute. The weird part was that he cared. If he was the ruthless jerk she'd expected, he would have just galloped off and left her to fend for herself.

She made sure not to reveal too much riding skill. Even giggled and pretended to drop the reins when Taffy reached for some grass by the side of the drive. After about five minutes of walking past scenic castle vistas, the horses were nicely warmed up and she had a feel for the lovely Taffy.

That's when they passed through one more gate and a solid mile of open fields stretched out before them like a racetrack. "Shall we let them stretch their legs?" She spoke innocently.

"Um." James looked doubtfully at the pair of them. She must appear to be very tiny up on Taffy, who was the biggest horse she'd ever sat on, at least eighteen hands. "Okay. You lead the way."

No doubt so he could come scoop her up when she fell off. She smiled secretly as she passed him. Then she gathered up her reins and urged Taffy into a collected trot. When she was sure the horse was listening to her and understood that she knew what she was doing, she sat down and squeezed with her legs. As anticipated, Taffy shifted gears like a finely tuned Bentley, easing into a steady canter, then an active one. She rose out of the saddle as Taffy opened up into a gallop, and realized she was grinning from ear to ear for reasons that had nothing to do with James, as the wind whipped her face and the landscape flew by in a green blur.

This was fun!

Four

James had planned to keep to a walk. He'd deliberately chosen Dougal, who was recovering from a tendon injury and needed to be eased back into work. Fiona was small and slight, and just because she'd gone on a beach ride once in her life did not mean she could ride. She looked rather precarious up on Taffy, whose powerful build was outmatched only by her gentle, forgiving nature. In her fashionable skinny jeans and white designer loafers, Fiona looked as if she should be strolling along a quay somewhere, not climbing astride a massive beast, but she kept smiling and managed to adjust her stirrups and girth like someone who knew what she was doing.

He kept things at a slow pace, which wasn't easy with poor, wound-up Dougal desperate to blow off some steam. He probably should have taken a quieter horse, but he knew Dougal needed the workout.

Then Fiona took off. Staring wide-eyed, he watched

after her, struggling passionately with Dougal, who wanted nothing more than to blast off after her but could not be allowed to because of his healing tendon. Rearing and throwing himself around, Dougal kept James fully occupied for a solid five minutes, until he heard the drumbeat of Taffy's hooves returning back toward him. He looked up, already reaching for his phone to call for help, sure the horse would be riderless. But that wasn't the case.

"You're alive." Relief crashed through him. Fiona's face shone, cheeks pink and lips reddened by the wind. Taffy was panting and blowing, stretching her neck down.

"I've fallen in love."

"Really?" He blinked, still struggling with Dougal, who had now wound himself into a frenzy. He was almost tempted to shout that he was in love, too. That kiss kept slamming back into his mind, which didn't help matters. Things couldn't get much crazier than they already were, and Fiona was like a blast of cool, fresh air in his rather predictable existence.

"Taffy is a horse in a million. She listens to every move you make."

He laughed. Okay. So she wasn't in love with him. Was he disappointed? He wanted to slap himself. "I know. That's why I chose her for you. She also ignores any stupid moves you make, but that doesn't seem to be important in your case." He scanned the horse and rider. She sat effortlessly on her huge mount, with a casual loose rein, as if she was lounging in a beach chair. "I admit I hadn't expected you to be so…competent."

"I know." She laughed. "You expected me to slide off when we started trotting, didn't you?"

"Absolutely." He grinned. "But I'm glad you didn't.

Dougal is recovering from an injury, so he and I are devastated that we can't join you in another gallop."

"Maybe another time." Her chin lifted and her face shining, she looked ravishingly beautiful, even in the black velvet riding hat that didn't flatter too many people.

"Definitely." In fact, he wasn't sure he could wait until tomorrow. "But perhaps for now we could stay together in a steady trot so poor Dougal doesn't bow another tendon."

"You've got it." She eased into a trot, and he watched her elegant behind rise up and down in the saddle, with the feeling that his tongue was hanging out like a dog's. Fiona Lam was turning out to be different than he expected. Was that good? He wasn't sure. He'd been instantly attracted to her, and that had grown into a rich and invigorating lust during the hours they'd spent together thus far.

She'd seemed a good prospect as a partner, as she was intelligent and appeared sensible. Her blend of Singaporean and American background held its own appeal, from a purely business perspective, since she bridged the two cultures where most of his business took place, and where he sometimes ran aground when his own very British upbringing put him at a disadvantage. Sometimes he didn't "get" other people's opinions and perspectives, and it made him realize how narrow the horizons he'd been raised with truly were.

So far Fiona's visit was a blistering success. He'd better make sure that cup base didn't turn up anytime soon as he had no intention of losing her. Not that they were likely to find it anyway. It had probably been melted down into a weapon or used as a target for shooting practice, knowing the Drummond clan. If it did happen to turn up, he could find some other way to delay her. She certainly seemed to be enjoying herself so far.

She slowed her trot and let him come alongside her. "I don't understand you at all."

"No?"

"You could do this every day, and you choose to live in a high-rise apartment in one of the most crowded cities on earth."

"I must be mad."

He'd brought women here before—they often clamored to come see the ancestral pile—and most of them spent their time complaining about the weather or wondering where the nearest good shopping was (answer: a very long way away). Fiona, on the other hand, had dived right into the spirit of the place.

"I think you are mad. That's okay, though. We're all mad in our own special way." She rode alongside him, grinning from ear to ear. "I'm beginning to think I've been crazy to spend so much of the past five years hunched over a laptop. I definitely need to spread my wings a bit."

"You've earned the right." She'd made more in her first five years out of college than most people made in a lifetime.

"I suppose I have. I never looked at it that way. I feel like a slacker when I'm not working on my next big plan."

"Believe me, I know all about that. I don't think I've taken a legitimate vacation in..." Had he ever taken one? He didn't even remember a ski trip that didn't have some ulterior business partnership motive. "A while."

"It appears that we have a lot in common."

"Yes." Desire snapped between them like the brisk hilltop wind. Thoughts of kissing her crowded his mind and made it hard to stay focused on Dougal's antics. Would it be so wrong if they made love tonight? The attraction was obviously mutual. They'd known each other more than twenty-four hours and had already spent one night under the same roof.

"Why are you laughing?" Her eyes sparkled and her hair whipped around her riding helmet.

"I don't know. I must be drunk on fresh air." He did feel giddy, possibilities swirling in his mind. Could he have found the right woman to marry? Of course he didn't love her or anything dramatic like that. He was far too sensible to let his emotions run amok. You didn't own a two-billion-dollar business if you let anything rule you other than a cool head. But his calculating mind was spitting out projections that made time with Fiona look like a very promising investment.

"Me, too." A drizzle of rain had joined the stiff wind and glossed her cheeks. Most women he knew would be squinting against it and worrying about their hairdo. Fiona tipped back her head and let the mist kiss her skin.

He had every intention of kissing her himself, as soon as possible. "We'd better go back. I think Dougal has had enough excitement for one morning."

"Of course. I'm dying to see more of the castle now that I've had a good night's sleep and my brain is functioning again. I barely even remember what happened yesterday."

He wanted to laugh again. That kiss was so fresh in his mind he could almost taste it. Was she trying to claim she was so addled by travel and lack of sleep that it had happened by accident? Strangely, that fueled his desire to seduce her all over again. He could rarely resist a challenge. "I wish I could race you back."

"I'd win." Confidence shone in her face, brighter than her wind-slapped pink cheeks.

"I know these horses a lot better than you. Maybe I deliberately gave you the slower one."

"I'm sure you did, but I'd win anyway."

"How?" Dougal started dancing under him, probably sensing his fierce desire to take her up on the challenge right this minute.

"Sheer determination. It will get you almost anything if you have enough of it."

He laughed. "We'll have to put that to the test."

"I'm looking forward to it."

So was he. She might think she could beat him, but that was only because he'd given her room to make that mistake. No one ever got the best of James Drummond unless he wanted them to for some strategic purpose of his own. If she beat him it was because he'd let her, for reasons she might never guess.

What would she think if she knew that he was planning their wedding? A grand affair in the old chapel on the estate, with guests flown in from all over the world. Then an ostentatious party in Singapore to woo future business partners and impress them with his new "family man" status. He'd plan and execute the entire affair like the rollout of a new business. Fiona Lam would have no idea what hit her.

The exhilarating morning ride left Fiona buzzing with excitement. She couldn't wait to do it again. Sadness sneaked in around the edges of her pleasure, since this adventure—like her mini-affair with James— would be short-lived. For a few brief seconds, astride her powerful and generous horse, she'd allowed herself to imagine what it would feel like if this was her real life. Her imagination had gone galloping off with her, and she'd had to reel it harshly back in. She was hardly cut out to be lady of a Scottish manor, and the locals would no doubt be appalled that a girl with no pedigree whatsoever had usurped their laird.

She wanted to laugh. She was planning to usurp their laird. No one here would ever even know about it, though. She'd get that factory back and disappear quietly to another part of the world. No one outside the insular business community of Singapore would ever even notice it had happened. For James it would be a small business plan gone sour, and soon forgotten. He'd forget her quickly enough, too.

She swallowed. How odd to know the ending of this story when it had barely started.

They spent the afternoon walking the halls of the older parts of the castle, through surprisingly small rooms with flagstone floors and plastered walls. "Where's all the stuff?"

"What stuff?" James had changed into dark pants and a pale striped shirt that added to his patrician air.

"The furniture, knick-knacks, you know. It doesn't look like anyone ever lived here."

"I suppose my ancestors probably gambled it all away or sold it off. Don't forget old uncle Gaylord, who lost the place in a card game. Maybe the person who won it put everything on the auction block."

"What a shame." The room they were in had a single high window, almost above eye level, which gave it the air of a prison cell. "It's part of your family history."

"The history exists regardless of whether there's a bunch of old junk here." He pointed to a dark soot stain on the ceiling. "Someone probably sat here reading by candlelight."

"Or sewing."

"Or gambling away their last shilling." His mischievous grin tickled her insides.

"Or plotting revenge on their enemies."

"Or making love." His eyes narrowed slightly, thoughtful.

"You don't need light for that," she said quietly. The atmosphere thickened.

"True. Just a soft surface." A tiny smile pulled at his mouth.

"If even that." She tried to act much cooler than she felt. Her imagination was scampering off in all directions. James Drummond spread-eagled on the flagstone floor, half-naked and whispering her name. James Drummond pressing her up against the plastered wall, breathing in her ear. "Maybe they weren't as picky as we are."

James stepped toward her and kissed her in one swift movement. Her breath and thoughts fled for parts unknown as his lips closed over hers. He tasted delicious, intoxicating as a fine Scotch whiskey, even though they hadn't drank a drop at lunch. His arms circled her torso, holding her close in a very romantic way. No groping or fondling—more's the pity, since her fingers now pressed into the muscle of his back and itched to roam farther afield.

When he pulled back she opened her eyes, blinking in the bright light coming through the high window. "Was that some kind of historical reenactment?" She didn't know what to say and just wanted to fill the air with sound to break the thick tension that had gathered.

"It's history now, but the future will be here before we know it." He tilted his head slightly, regarding her through narrowed, storm-gray eyes. His arms still held her, and the desire to break free warred with the urge to clutch him closer. What was she doing? Could this lead *anywhere* good?

Oh, yes, some dark, selfish and lustful part of her brain answered. Somewhere very good. James's bed, for a start.

She'd been so wrapped up in her business lately she'd had little time for socializing. The publicity leading up to the sale of Smileworks had scared all but her oldest and closest friends into being intimidated by her, and the fact that it had sold for more than her wildest dreams hadn't helped one bit.

She blinked again. James was far too good-looking for his own good or anyone else's. How was a girl supposed to keep her cool around him?

She wished she could give her dad some money and he could buy himself a new factory. Then she wouldn't have to worry about getting the old one back from James. Her dad wouldn't take money. She knew it. He'd be angry and feel as if she was lording it over him. He was proud to a fault, and then some. She didn't care though. It just made her want to try harder to make him happy. She was proud, too, one of the many traits she'd inherited from him.

Which made it rather awkward to stand here wrapped in James Drummond's powerful arms. She wondered if anyone had ever kissed their enemy before in this very room.

Quite probably. "What does the future hold?" She looked into his face, which wasn't easy since he was more than half a head taller than her.

"I'm no fortune-teller." Those dark eyes seemed to peer into her soul, which shrank from their penetrating gaze. "I can only see what's right in front of me."

Then he kissed her again, harder this time. Stars flashed behind her eyelids—simple chemistry, nothing more, she reassured herself. Thick, hot lust surged inside her. Again, just chemistry. And that was the only thing making her fingers creep lower, toward the waistband of his pants, where she was absolutely not going to grope the well-muscled backside she'd enjoyed such impressive views of during their ride that morning.

He was deliberately seducing her. His lips trailed over her cheek, leaving her skin hot and flushed. His fingers now skated up and down her spine. His hips jutted toward her, and she could feel his arousal thick and hard behind the civilized veneer of clothing.

A civilized veneer that was in real danger of being ripped right off.

"Stop!" She squeaked the word as she managed to pull back from the kiss.

"You don't mean that." His voice was low, throaty, his gaze amused.

You're right, I don't. "I've just met you. I'm here as your prisoner—I mean, your guest—and things are moving too fast."

"My prisoner?" A dark brow rose slightly.

"Freudian slip." She lifted her chin, which helped her see eye to eye with him. Why did he have to be so tall? "But you have to admit that I can't easily escape."

"So much the better." His arms still held firm around her waist.

"Is this how you treat all your guests?" Frustrated desire snapped through her like stray current, making her edgy. She didn't like the way he could just pick her up and play with her as if she were a toy. And she especially didn't like the way she responded so instantly and totally.

"No. Only the pretty ones."

"Then your reputation is well earned."

He froze. She felt his hands still and his muscles grow hard. Her own chest constricted as she realized that she'd revealed too much. She wasn't supposed to know anything about him. "What do you know of my reputation?"

"I did ask around before volunteering to travel several thousand miles to stay with a virtual stranger." Good save. Of course that's what any sensible person would do.

"But apparently you came anyway." His fierce gaze made her stomach clench.

"I'm not afraid of a…rake."

He laughed. "A rake? What is this, the eighteenth century?"

"I couldn't think of a more polite word. Okay, how about a playa?"

He grinned. "I'm not sure anyone's called me that, either. And I'm not the playboy that people make out. I never, ever date more than one woman at a time."

"So why haven't you ever married?" She couldn't resist re-asking the bold question. It was the perfect moment to dig a little deeper beneath James's cool facade. And his tormenting arms were no longer wrapped around her, so she could breathe again. "I know you said you haven't met the right woman, but I know there's more to it than that. And since I'm apparently already on your embarrassing list of statistics, you might as well tell me."

He frowned. "I did meet the right woman, once."

The words hung in the air and bounced off the bare walls. Then he turned and strode for the door.

Fiona hurried after him, suddenly sure that what had

happened with this woman could be the key to James Drummond's heart. Did she dump him mercilessly? Run off with his best friend? Her heart beat faster as she rushed along the corridor. James was heading deeper into the unused parts of the castle, past more closed doors. "Where are we going?"

He didn't answer. Maybe lost in his own thoughts.

"Who was she?" She didn't want to miss her chance to ask about his lost love. The right opportunity might never come up again. She already couldn't believe that he'd mentioned her, when he seemed so guarded about his personal life.

The long hallway ended in a stone wall, with stone stairs going up to the right and down to the left. James went up. "Her name was Catriona." He took the stairs two at a time.

Fiona climbed after him. "Sounds Scottish."

"She was." He reached the top of the flight of stairs and disappeared out of sight.

"Was? Did she die?" She assumed she was dead to James, not really deceased, so his answer caught her by surprise.

"She did. Seventeen years ago this weekend."

"I'm so sorry." Emotion slapped her hard. She'd been digging at him, trying to extract information for her own purposes, and she'd hit upon a raw vein of pain.

"Why? You didn't kill her."

He swung around and his face was dark. "I did."

She swallowed. Were there ugly truths about James Drummond that made his fearsome reputation as a businessman seem like child's play? And she was all alone in the deserted wing of a remote Scottish castle with him. She hadn't even told her friends she was coming. She was sure they'd think she was crazy and try to talk her out of it, especially if she told them her underhanded purpose in being James's guest.

Her gut told her to trust him, though. In fact, it begged her to throw her arms around him and offer some kind of compassion for what was obviously a seventeen-year-old emotional burden he still carried with him. "What happened?" She asked the question softly.

His brow had smoothed and his composure returned. "It was a car accident."

"Oh." Relief swept through her that it was something so prosaic. "And you were driving?"

"Yes." He looked up. "How did you know?"

"I guessed. You feel guilty."

"I am guilty. I should have avoided the accident."

"Did it happen near here?" She realized she was hugging herself.

"Just a few miles outside the village." He shoved a hand through his hair. She prayed he would tell her more so she didn't have to ask any more insensitive-sounding questions. "It was late at night and we were driving back from a party. I was taking her to her family's house in town."

A local girl. That surprised her. For some reason she'd assumed James would date only women from more predictably glamorous locales. "Had you known each other long?"

"Our whole lives." He looked up and inhaled sharply. "We were both away at boarding school most of the time, of course, but on every holiday we spent as much time together as we could. Her father was—is—the local doctor, and he would drop her off here every morning on the way to begin his rounds so we could spend the day riding or arguing about books."

"Sounds like you were best friends."

"Oh, we were, and as we grew into our teenage years we were more than that."

"She was your first love."

"My only love." He said it quite fast, and she wondered if he was saying it for the first time. She shivered slightly. A few moments ago they'd been kissing and holding each other, but now a gulf as wide as the castle battlements had opened between them. "I did love her." He was looking out an opening in the stone wall. They stood on a sort of stone landing between floors, and the window looked out onto a blanket of lush green fields, dotted with sheep and ringed by dark, uncultivated hills.

"And that's why you've never been able to love anyone else?"

He didn't answer right away, but she saw him frown. "I never grew that close to anyone else." He stared out the window. "But maybe I'm finally ready to move on."

A cool flush of shock froze her to the spot. Was he telling her that he might be ready to "move on" with her, after seventeen years of pining, even though they'd only just met?

Guilt stabbed her hard. She wasn't here to mend his broken heart, but to mend her father's. She hadn't given any thought to James's feelings at all, mostly because she'd assumed he didn't have any. How could he possibly think she might be "the one" he'd managed to avoid for so long?

Or maybe she was reading too much into the situation. He could have brought her here just to entertain himself while he prepared his search for the perfect lady of the manor. Probably someone tall and blond, with aristocratic ancestry traceable back to the Bronze Age.

Certainly not a petite, Californian business geek with an evil scheme up her sleeve.

She had no idea what to say. The atmosphere had thickened as if a storm was gathering, but the white sky outside was as mute as the castle ghosts. "That's great. It's been a long time." She cursed herself for sounding so lame. And as if she might expect him to "move on" with her.

"So they tell me. Sometimes it feels like only yesterday. Especially when I come back here." He frowned and headed up the flight of stairs. She followed him with relief that she could move and breathe again.

"That's why you don't like to come back here, isn't it?"

"Yes."

So he'd avoided his ancestral home and its stunning natural surroundings not because he thought the place was boring and remote, but because it was haunted by memories and regrets that time hadn't managed to erase. "I bet she would have wanted you to move on." She wasn't even sure why she said it. It seemed the kind of thing an elderly aunt might suggest, not a girl brought here to distract him from his painful past.

He turned and frowned, then laughed. "How would you know?"

She felt insulted, as if he'd slapped her, which made her protest quickly. "If she loved you, she'd want you to be happy." Unless she was selfish and heartless and wanted him to spend the rest of his life pining for her, which was entirely possible, of course.

He was silent, climbing the stone stairs slowly. What floor were they on? She felt as if they'd climbed enough stairs to be at the top of a skyscraper by now. They reached another landing, and he turned a heavy iron latch and opened an arched wooden door. She gasped as it opened to the outside and light poured into the dim stairwell. James stepped outside and she followed him onto a terrace, high above the surrounding countryside.

"You're right, of course." The wind carried his words away. "She would have been disgusted by my behavior."

"Why?"

"Letting innocent women think that I'm an ordinary man who might make them happy." He squinted at the bright horizon, brown crumpled peaks against the stark white sky, with a carpet of lush green pasture beneath. "Only to leave them as soon as they showed any sign of emotion."

Fiona swallowed. He certainly wasn't advertising his better qualities to her. Which likely meant that he wasn't too interested in impressing her or having any kind of relationship beyond a quick kiss and grope. Why did that make her gut twist in such an uncomfortable way? She shouldn't care at all. She wasn't looking to fall madly in love with James and have him pledge his undying adoration for her.

"So how do you feel different now?" She asked the probing question, almost daring him to insult her more. She still didn't fully understand why he'd asked her here. She didn't believe he'd brought her to find the cup, as he didn't seem to care too much about it one way or the other. Besides, she was no seasoned treasure hunter—unless the treasure was consumer dollars.

Instead of softening, his face hardened, cheekbones and proud nose and chin forming an impressive silhouette against the bright sky. "It's time for me to choose a wife and produce an heir."

Her already churning gut tightened. She straightened her shoulders and took in a deep breath. He was obviously playing with her, and it was downright rude to kiss her then tell her he was ready to marry someone else. She lifted a brow. "Do you have anyone in mind?"

He looked right at her, and she was shocked to see his gray eyes so dark with emotion. "I do."

Five

Fiona stood openmouthed for what felt like a full minute. Had James just intimated that *she* might be his future wife and the mother of the next Drummond heir? She was the only woman there and, polite to a fault, James Drummond was hardly the type to smooch her then discuss his plans to marry another woman. Maybe he was really impressed with her riding!

No, she must be imagining things. All this unaccustomed fresh air had fogged her mind. "I hope you do find love." She had no idea what else to say. She couldn't ignore such a dramatic pronouncement. "It would be a shame for this place to have no one to inherit it."

"I know, it would get bought by American investors and turned into a golf resort." Mischief gleamed in his eyes and sent another spark of attraction flashing through her.

"Maybe that wouldn't be so bad?" she countered, one eyebrow raised.

"Not if you like golf, I suppose."

"This certainly is a million-dollar view."

"I'd want a lot more than that for it." He surveyed the impressive landscape. You could see literally for miles in every direction. The village lay about half a mile from the castle, but if there were other buildings out there they were well hidden and invisible.

"I don't blame you. It's like owning your own country, except without the trouble of citizens."

"Or the bother of modern conveniences like shops."

"Bah, who needs 'em. I order everything online anyway. I'd be quite happy in my own little kingdom." Her statement was bold, considering where this conversation had already gone. Rash, even, but it seemed to lighten the serious mood. If he was teasing her with the prospect of marriage, then why not call his bluff?

"Really?" He turned to face her, leaning against the castle battlements. "You don't think you'd get bored, or lonely?"

"Nope." She lifted her chin. "I'm pretty sure I could keep myself entertained 24/7. And there's plenty of room for a helipad here if I needed to ensure a quick getaway."

He laughed. "There's one here already. My father had it built in the 1970s. It fell into disuse after his helicopter disappeared at sea."

"I'm so sorry. That must have been terrible."

"The worst part was that I never really got to know him. He was away a lot when I was little, then I went off to boarding school around the time I was old enough to hold a conversation. I suppose I would have missed him more if we'd been close, but it is frustrating that I never had the chance."

I know how you feel. In fact, she felt it literally in her gut. How sad that he should have missed out on getting to know his father as she did, even though it was for different reasons. At least she still had the chance to make things right.

"Where does your mother live?" she asked with some trepidation, hoping she hadn't been killed in the same crash.

"She lives in Zurich. My mother rarely even came here when I was growing up, since she can't stand the place and hasn't set foot in it for decades. I suspect she'd believe in the supposed curse. The whole estate gave her the chills. She always said she couldn't bear to be so far from civilization."

Fiona frowned. "I don't feel that at all. I think it's peaceful."

"It is peaceful in a lonely way, because there's no one to disturb the peace."

"Maybe that's why you brought me here?"

"Quite possibly." A wry smile pulled at his lips again. "And so far it's working very well."

He was about one foot of brisk Scottish air away from her, but she could swear that heat rolled between them. The wind, and their ride, had brought color to his cheeks and a sparkle to his eyes that made them seem far less cold. Excitement prickled inside her. Would they kiss again? Where would this lead?

She'd never been in such a strange situation before. Maybe this is what happened to people who sold their business and became wealthy overnight. Men certainly didn't sweep her off to their foreign estates when she was a slightly geeky product designer and wannabe en-

trepreneur. In fact, she'd gone for long periods without
a single date. If she hadn't done independent research
into James's finances for her own nefarious purposes,
she'd be tempted to assume that he wanted to marry her
for money to fix up his money pit of an estate. Since
she knew better, she couldn't for the life of her figure
out what he was up to.

An electronic tone interrupted her thoughts, and
James reached into his pocket. When he pulled out a
phone, she realized this was the first time she'd seen
him take a call since they'd been together. She didn't
even realize he had one on him.

She turned away to give him some privacy, though
her ears remained pricked. Who was privileged enough
to phone James away from the office? He must have
someone intercepting his calls somewhere, as a man
with his fingers in so many pies must get a lot of phone
calls. Who was his assistant? She should really know
this stuff by now, but it was hard to find information
about James Drummond that wasn't public knowledge.

His conversation was a low murmur, but he was definitely talking to a man. She could tell from the gruff,
rather formal manner. After a few minutes, he told the
caller that he looked forward to seeing him, and then
hung up.

"I didn't know you carried a phone."

"I wish I didn't, but the world expects you to be available at all hours these days. My assistant screens all my
calls. And this was a man I have an interesting project
in the works with."

"In Singapore?" Her stomach started fluttering. Was
this the project that had required him to grab her dad's
business?

"Yes, among other places."

"Let me guess, a chain of hotels?" She wanted to know more without actually asking.

"Not exactly." His face was a smooth granite mask, as usual, and she could tell that was all the information she would get. Would James Drummond ever kiss and tell? There was really only one way to find out.

"I'm afraid I have to go sit in front of a computer for a while. Some figures to go over. Do feel free to explore the place."

They walked down the stairs and back toward the inhabited part of the castle. James was obviously preoccupied, and he wasn't the type to fill the air with noise just to be polite. Her brain was busy, too, wondering exactly what would happen after dinner that night. She no longer had the excuse of being exhausted from their flight, and James had already put some pretty impressive moves on her.

Not that she'd resisted too hard.

Back in her room, she phoned her best friend, Crystal, in San Diego.

"What do you mean you're in Scotland?"

"It all happened so fast I didn't have time to fill you in."

"I've wanted to go there for years. I can't believe you went without me."

"It wasn't a planned thing. James invited me and I couldn't think of a good way to say no."

"James? Not James from chem class."

She laughed, remembering the short kid with the acne and the calculator in his hip pocket. "Not even close. This one's a Scottish laird."

"Holy guacamole, you're going to be a duchess."

"I think duchesses are English."

"Well, whatever they have in Scotland, then. A laird-ess."

"I am not. I only just met him and there's absolutely nothing going on between us." She froze when she realized she'd lied to her best friend since third grade. "Okay, so we kissed once. Or twice. But other than that it's kind of a business thing."

"A business thing with kisses? Intriguing. And not your style at all. Didn't you once refuse to kiss Danny Fibonacci because you thought he wanted to steal your lemonade stand corner?"

"Since he's recently been accused of insider trading, I think I was right on the money."

Crystal laughed. "What kind of business are you doing?"

"Looking for an old cup. Or a piece of one." She frowned. Sometimes it was hard to keep her mind on that part of this whole adventure. She had to remember that was supposedly the real reason she'd come to Scotland with a virtual stranger. "It's a family heirloom that went missing three hundred years ago."

"Sounds like a really lame excuse for him to seduce you into his lair."

"Hey! I have my own reasons for being here."

"Let me guess, there's three of them—tall, dark and handsome."

She glanced around the room, hoping there wasn't a hidden camera somewhere, or a bug. "Not in the least. Well, he is. But I'm here because he managed to swindle my father's factory away from him and I'm trying to figure out a way to get it back."

She felt relieved to get her skullduggery off her chest. Crystal did not offer reassuring encouragement, however. In fact, there was a long silence at the other end of the line. "How are things going with your dad?" Her voice sounded...wary.

"Great. He's pretty upset about losing his business, but all I have to do is figure out why James wanted it so badly, then I can work out how to get it back."

"James, huh? Have you tried buying it back?"

"He said no when I had a Realtor ask him. But if I get to know him I might find a better strategy."

"What if he still says no?"

She bit her lip. She hadn't really thought how she might proceed if he downright refused to part with the factory. She suspected a businessman like James would always have his price. "I'll find a way. I have a lot of money."

"This situation does not sound good. How do you know your dad would even appreciate what you're doing? You barely know him."

Crystal's comment stung like a slap. "I've been spending a lot of time with him."

"He could have come and visited you in California when you were a kid. But he chose not to."

"It's complicated." Every year she'd hoped and prayed for a visit and imagined it in her mind. She begged her mom to take her to Singapore, but it was too expensive. Every year there had been excuses. She knew her mom and dad had had a very bitter divorce, and she suspected her mom just wanted to forget he ever existed.

No more. Now she could finally share her birthday with her dad, or phone him just to say hi the way she'd always dreamed.

"I think it's great that you're trying to reach out to your dad, and I know you mean well, Fi, but I don't want to see you get hurt."

"I can take care of myself, thank you." She wished she hadn't called Crystal in the first place. "In the meantime, I'm having an interesting vacation in Scotland."

"It certainly sounds that way. I can't wait to hear more juicy details as they occur."

Since she now knew that dinner was an elegant affair served by waitstaff in the magnificent oak-paneled dining room, she donned a black knee-length dress and put on a pair of pearl earrings—smart, but not too over the top. Thank goodness for the little black dress.

Anticipation flickered in her nerves and muscles as she applied lipstick and eyeliner. Two kisses already meant that a third was a virtual certainty. While a casual observer might think this could make it easier to ask him to sell her the factory, she couldn't help thinking that it made the situation way more complicated and awkward. Especially since he had no idea she'd ever even heard of the factory.

A knock on the door made her suck in a breath. "Come in."

The door swung open. "Dinner's ready." James stood in the doorway, elegant as usual in a dark jacket and pants, with a crisp pale shirt. How odd that they were both dressed up to eat dinner at home with no guests. This truly was a different world.

"You look beautiful." His slow, steady gaze swept from her head to her black Manolo slingbacks.

"Thanks. You're cute, too." She resisted the urge to giggle. This felt like a date, with great expectations. When she was with James, it seemed natural to flirt a little with him. Even the kissing didn't feel strange. Not until later when she was alone and trying to get her plans back on track.

Tonight's mission: let him know she wanted a piece of property in Singapore in the exact location where the factory was. "I'm almost ready." She pretended to touch up her lipstick. She didn't want to seem as if she was jumping to attention too quickly. Better to act casual and nonchalant, as if nothing really mattered much.

"Any time you take is obviously well spent." The appreciation in his eyes heated her skin from across the room. It made her feel beautiful. Which was weird because she wasn't used to feeling more than, well, above average. She tried to look smart, and she was blessed with a trim body, but her looks weren't really…va-va-voom. Men didn't usually turn their heads or spill their drinks when she entered a room.

But James made her feel as if that could happen.

"Do you always eat sitting at that big table with people waiting on you hand and foot?"

"When I'm here, yes."

"Don't you ever want to eat in front of the TV or something?" She walked past him out of the room. Heat rose through her as their bodies drew close.

"I might, but I don't. Tradition. And the staff here have little enough to do. I don't want them all feeling neglected and handing in their notice."

"Now you're thinking like a businessman."

"This estate is more of a business than a home to me."

He walked a step behind her, and she shivered slightly when she felt his hand settle into the small of her back. "That's sad when you think of how many people must have lived—and died—here. Each room and piece of furniture has so much history."

"Some of the many reasons why I like my new-build condo in Singapore." He caught up with her and she saw his wicked smile. "I can relax without being surrounded by people—living or dead—with expectations."

She frowned, partly because her attention had settled on a huge painting of a young man next to a stag, in a woodland setting. The painting filled the end of the corridor and was over life-size. From the man's clothing she could tell it was eighteenth century. "That painting is stunning."

"I suppose so. All I notice is the way his eyes follow you as you walk past."

She squinted at it. "But he's looking off to the side."

"Not the man. The stag." He swung sideways and headed down the stairs. She paused for a moment. The stag was staring right at her with big, liquid brown eyes. "Goodness." She hurried after him. "I see what you mean. There's a lot of pressure coming from different directions." She glanced over her shoulder to see if the giant beast was still watching her. He was. "What did you say the family motto was, again?"

"Keep your blade sharp." He grimaced slightly. "Good advice in the business world."

"At least you can cut your losses quickly with a sharp blade." She was trying to lighten the mood, but James stopped and stared at her.

"Yes, you can." Then he frowned and continued down the stairs.

As expected, dinner was an elegant repast at the long, polished table. She asked him questions about managing the estate, partly to learn more about him but mostly because she was burning with curiosity about how such an archaic endeavor worked in the twenty-first century.

"So the estate is self-supporting?" It was hard to believe the thousands of sheep that kept the grass neatly mowed also paid most of the bills.

"Only just. The market in organic wool fluctuates from season to season. I've been told the next step is to start producing our own luxury products, sweaters and such, but I don't have the appetite for that kind of business."

"Why not?"

"Not enough volume. The luxury business is all about producing and selling small amounts of goods with a high margin. That's not scalable enough to pique my interest."

"But you own luxury hotels and buildings. Surely that's similar."

"Nope." He sipped his wine. "In addition to collecting income from wealthy lovers of luxury, you are also sitting on a long-term gold mine. My grandfather's mantra was 'never sell the land!' and I've taken that to heart. The land is where true value lies, long-term."

Fiona cut her roast beef, heart pounding. She was already pretty sure he'd jumped on her father's factory for the land under it. What would he want with an outdated garment factory? How would she convince him to part with that land if his personal beliefs told him to clutch it to his chest? "Surely you sometimes sell property."

"Hardly ever." He smiled. "At least not yet. I suppose there might always be a price I couldn't resist."

She smiled back, already feeling a tingle of relief. "Would it have to be a very high price?"

"Oh, yes. Something more than money." He leaned back in his chair. "And I'd never part with this place, of course. No matter how much I sometimes want to."

"That would be like selling your own DNA."

"I'd part with my own DNA sooner. Let them use it

for research purposes. My cells will make more DNA." He'd finished eating and simply sat, watching her.

She put down her knife and fork. It was time to take her plan to the next level. Butterflies danced in her stomach, which didn't go well with the roast beef and Yorkshire pudding. "Something more than money." She raised a brow, hoping it looked flirtatious rather than accusatory. "Like a dare, perhaps?"

He tilted his head, obviously intrigued. "I can't say anyone's ever made an offer like that. I might have to consider it."

She worked hard to keep her breathing steady. She didn't want to move too fast and have him put the pieces together. "Well, I am looking for a new project. Since you obviously have a keen eye for opportunity, I'm thinking I should steal one of your cunning ideas for my next business."

He laughed. "I suspect you can come up with something far more interesting on your own."

"Maybe. Maybe not. Your expertise might be a complement to mine and produce something better than either of us could do alone." It wasn't easy to think business with James looking right at her with unconcealed desire in his gaze. Worse yet, his striking good looks and sharp mind made arousal bubble up inside her and no doubt gleam very obviously in her eyes. "You've already built a firm foothold in Singapore, for example, whereas I'm new to the place and still trying to figure it out."

"Singapore is on the cutting edge of the known world." He obviously appreciated her interest in his chosen home away from home. "A meeting place for minds and products from all over the world."

"Every container ship filled with goods has to pass right by it, due to simple quirks of geography."

His eyes sparkled. "Exactly. Until someone invents hovering aircraft to carry container loads of goods, it will continue to be the preeminent international gateway."

"Hmm." She pretended to chew her lip thoughtfully. "Maybe I should get back to work on my goods-transportation aircraft plan."

"I'd be the first to invest."

Or try to steal my business. She managed to keep a straight face. "But as you said, I don't have an appetite for that kind of business. I enjoy spotting trends and defining style. I think my next step will be into retail." Her brain was running like a sprinter. She'd visited her dad's old factory, which was a dated and decrepit one-story building on a down-at-heel street, only one block away from a glittering retail strip. It would be a fantastic spot for a hotel, but she couldn't fake an entry into that realm. Too far away from where she was now. "I've learned a lot about branding and creating something hip from my decal business, and I thought I might dip my toes into the fashion industry."

"Creating product, or reselling someone else's?"

"Maybe both, with a strong internet presence and a flagship store in Singapore." On the exact spot where her father's factory stood. "I have a lot of ideas for the clothing, so I want to start by finding the right space for my store."

She hoped her nose wasn't growing. Her blood pressure was certainly rising, along with that infuriating pulse of arousal that kept surging through her whenever their eyes met. If only they hadn't kissed already! It was painful to remember how quickly and totally her body had responded to his. Chemistry, that's all it was. Something that could be replicated in a lab and probably switched on and off at will in a group of unwitting test mice. She could control it, and even use it to her advantage.

"I certainly know Singapore well enough to suggest some ideal locations. We'll have to walk around together next time we're there."

"Excellent."

James took Fiona's hand and led her into the library. He'd sent the staff away early, to ensure them total privacy. He had a strong sense of something important and momentous about to happen. "Would you like a drink?"

"If you're having one." She smiled and sat on the wide leather sofa. She was being too polite and he could tell she still felt uncomfortable in the unfamiliar environment. He wanted to put her at ease.

"Champagne is good for every occasion, in my opinion. Let's celebrate the birth of your next business venture." He pulled a bottle from the fridge concealed behind wood paneling.

"Isn't that somewhat premature?" She crossed her shapely legs, sending a jolt of heat to his groin.

"Not at all. The most important part of a new business is the idea. Once you have that, everything can grow organically from there."

"So now I just need to add fertilizer and water?" She smiled as she took the champagne flute.

"Exactly." He sat next to her. The hairs on his thighs prickled with sensation at being so close to her. There was something different about Fiona. She didn't simper and coo and flirt as so many girls he met did. She was serious and thoughtful and funny. And very beautiful.

She raised her chin as she tilted her glass, and desire swelled inside him as her soft pink mouth closed around the glass. He longed to feel her lips pressed to his again. Arousal had throbbed inside him like a dull ache all afternoon, and he'd determined not to act on it again. He'd already moved too fast, and he didn't want to scare her off.

She might be the one.

Excitement flashed in his chest at the thought. Could he finally be about to choose a partner and start a family? It didn't seem possible. He'd told himself for so long that it wasn't meant to be. Since he'd met Fiona suddenly all his thoughts had shifted and rearranged themselves like furniture in a house that'd been redecorated by a keen-eyed designer. Things that seemed pointless, foolish and impossible just a week ago now gleamed with exciting possibilities.

And he had to be careful not to blow it.

Her dark hair, shiny and silky, swung forward as she placed her glass on the coffee table. He wanted to run his fingers through it. But he resisted and took another sip of champagne. "How did you learn to ride?" Another delicious surprise.

"The same way everyone else does. I took lessons." She smiled. "I'm rusty now. Haven't even sat on a horse for a couple of years."

"You certainly handled Taffy like a pro."

"Taffy was a very gracious host. I felt like a medieval princess up on such a huge horse, galloping through a remote landscape. I can't wait to do it again."

"Neither can I." Riding with Fiona was one more item on a rapidly unfurling list of things he couldn't wait to do. But kissing her had risen to the top.

One kiss, no more. He had to be a gentleman. She

was his guest and despite their sudden intimacy, they'd known each other only a few days. The wait would be well worthwhile if she were as perfect for him as he'd begun to suspect.

Before he had time to think it through, his mouth met hers. Heat flashed over him as he drew her close, finally giving in to the urge that had bedeviled him since their kiss earlier that day. The scent of her drove him insane, and he had no idea why. Her slim, athletic body felt sensational in his arms, and before he knew it one of his hands was exploring her well-toned thigh and backside, and a raw shudder of lust rippled through him.

She kissed him back with passion that stoked the flames ripping and rising inside him. He could feel her hands tugging at his shirt, and he gasped with pleasure as her cool fingers met the skin of his back. Before he knew it his own fingers had caught hold of the zipper on the back of her dress and were exploring the soft skin beneath it.

Get a grip, James.

But he couldn't. Fiona's hands now wandered into his waistband, making him inhale sharply as his erection thickened. She sighed in his ear, a soft, sweet sound that made all sensible thoughts fly from his brain. *Oh, Fiona.* He wasn't sure if he said the words aloud or not. Reality seemed very far away, though he was keenly aware of helping her out of the fitted black dress that hugged her trim curves so enticingly.

Naked on the sofa except for her sleek black bra and panties, she was an unbearable temptation, desire shining in her dark brown eyes and a flush of arousal darkening her cheeks.

She unbuttoned his shirt and tugged it off, then licked his chest in a way that made him groan unexpectedly. He returned the favor by removing her bra and letting his tongue explore the sweet curve of her breasts and the elegant arch of her neck.

Her fingers sent shock waves of heat traveling through him everywhere he touched, and his erection was now rock hard. As she helped him out of his pants, he knew this was heading in one direction and one direction only.

"We need a condom," he managed to rasp, clinging to the last shreds of common sense. He knew he had some in his bedroom, but that seemed a thousand miles away.

"Don't worry. I have it covered." She didn't hesitate for a second, her hands now tugging at his underwear and releasing his very obvious arousal. Her mouth moved over his erection, and he wondered if he was going to lose consciousness entirely as she licked and sucked him into a state of near madness.

Her body was both soft and firm, enticing and athletic, and he ached to wrap himself around it and sink in.

Which he did.

Fiona's sweet sighs almost undid him as he entered her as gently as he could. She responded immediately, lifting her hips and joining with him in a rhythm that started out slow and deliberate, like a waltz, then grew more and more frantic and frenzied, a crazy tango, until they were shifting positions and pressing their skin against every part of the sofa in an effort to prolong and sustain the intense and erotic pleasure that flowed between them.

It took every ounce of his honor, manhood and self-control to hold back until Fiona climaxed, then he let go with a sense of relief he'd never felt before. They crashed together onto the now-sticky leather and held each other tight, gasping and groaning and soaking in the waves of incredible pleasure.

She's the one.

He knew it as he knew his own name. He didn't love her, or anything so simple and prosaic as that. He didn't even know what love was. But he knew he could spend his life with this woman. Something about her touched a raw nerve deep inside him, and obviously tapped a rich vein of desire. So much for his silent pledges to be a gentleman.

He laughed.

"What's so funny?"

"I was going to keep my hands off you tonight."

"You failed miserably."

"I know. And that doesn't happen often. I must be losing my mind." He kissed her soft cheek, pleasure and happiness swelling in his heart.

"That's okay with me." She whispered the words in his ear as she trailed a tempting finger down below his belly button. He shuddered as desire rolled through him like a clap of thunder.

Will you marry me?

He knew better than to say it right now. At least he still had that much self-control. But tomorrow?

Six

Fiona woke up wondering where she was. Bright moonlight poured through a crack in the curtains and memories of the previous evening flooded back, making her stomach clench.

She'd slept with James Drummond.

A quick glance at the pillow next to her contradicted her thoughts. Nope. They hadn't slept together. They'd had hot steamy, passionate, uninhibited sex on a leather sofa in the library of his baronial castle. Then they'd quietly gone to their separate rooms to sleep.

What had she been thinking? It was one thing to kiss him, quite another to rip his clothes off with wild abandon and make the beast with two backs, shortly after figuring out how to trick him into selling her a property she wanted. He had no idea who she was or that she was here for a form of revenge.

Should she be proud of herself for successfully seducing James into a false sense of security? Maybe some people would be, but she felt disgusted by her own duplicity. The worst part was that she actually liked James. To her horror she found him rather sweet, oddly affectionate and passionate in a way she'd never expected.

Her own feelings surprised her. Was it her treasonous purpose here that charged the atmosphere with sexual tension and sent desire whipping through her body at every glance?

She didn't think so.

In one of the universe's cruel little jokes, she suspected that she and James actually had a lot in common and shared a fierce physical attraction based on simple and natural chemistry. In other words, they were a good match.

What a shame he was going to end up hating her when he found out she'd come here for her own reasons.

She picked up her phone to check the time. 4:30 a.m.? Ugh. There was a message, so she replayed it, hoping for a distraction.

"Fifi, I'm worried about you." Her father's gruff voice. She smiled. How sweet of him to think about her. "Don't let that devil James Drummond take advantage of you." She blanched. Though had James really taken advantage of her, or was it the other way around? Either way, her dad would be horrified. "You can't get the factory back. You should come home."

The abrupt beep at the end of the message made her jump. He wanted her to come back to Singapore and thought of it as her home? Her heart swelled. Just a few weeks ago he'd never have thought to call her. How much their relationship had changed already! Soon she'd be helping him rebuild his business and his pride and they'd embrace a bright future together.

It would be midday in Singapore. Should she call him to reassure him? Or would she just feel more deceptive when she told him everything was fine while her insides still throbbed with sense memories of last night?

The thought of lying there wide-awake for another three or four hours made her want to run around screaming, so she dialed his number.

"Fifi, you need to come home." His immediate command made her smile.

"Hi, Dad. Don't worry about me. I'm enjoying Scotland."

"That's what I'm worried about!"

She wanted to laugh, except that his worries were well-founded. "James has no idea who I am, so don't fret. I'll be back before you know it." Her mind tried to crank out new possibilities that could contain this mess somewhat. "What about if I help you find a new building for your factory?"

"Bah. I'm too old to start again."

"Nonsense. You're not even sixty! I could help you figure out a new business plan. It would be fun." Then she wouldn't have to worry about tricking James and they could start all over again on a different footing. She could buy her father a factory in a far more sensible industrial area with much lower taxes, and he could rebuild his business, with her emotional and financial support. "That wasn't a good spot for a factory, anyway. The neighborhood got too fancy."

"That's what made it valuable. I was going to sell that land and make my fortune."

Then you should have paid your taxes. She held her tongue. The taxes had spiraled out of control as the value of the land rose, and her dad had stubbornly clung to the factory when his profits no longer covered the expenses. He was one of the few people who failed to benefit from Singapore's rapid growth as a world business center. "Why don't you try a different kind of business? What about another restaurant?" He'd had a chain of steakhouses or something similar. At least that's what her mom said.

"No thanks. Customers give me a bellyache."

She laughed. Her dad's people skills did not seem to be that great. She could imagine him barking at anyone who dared to complain about the food. "What about something that services hotels or shipping so you're cashing in on the new economy?"

"Handbags and shoes made me a rich man, Fifi. They're what I know and what I like."

Her heart sank. He was so stubborn. Apparently getting his accursed factory back was the only way to make him happy, and he obviously did want it, no matter what he said. Even though making dated handbags that couldn't compete with Chinese exports sounded like a sinkhole for money.

Unless… Maybe she could help him with rebranding and bring to life the high-end luxury retail store she'd made up to humor James. Now she did laugh. Was her little white lie the way to make everyone happy? "I know, Dad. It's what you love. I get it, and I'll make sure you get it back."

"You're a daughter any man would be proud of. Come home soon, Fifi." Characteristically abrupt, he hung up, leaving her listening to a dial tone with a mix of confusion and happiness. Okay, so the situation was complicated. She'd just have to negotiate it the best way she could. If only she could give her dad the money.

But he was a man of fierce convictions who held tightly to what he believed, and she admired that. She wanted him to feel the same way about her, and all this would be worth it in the end when she could stand arm in arm with her dad, both of them successful again and with a bright future to share.

James felt a twinge of unaccustomed anxiety as he walked across the gravel and up the steps. His early-morning conviction and enthusiasm was fired by their unbelievably sensual night. A day of rushing around and trying to make things happen had slapped him back to reality. By the time he finally contacted and visited a jeweler who could make and size a ring to his exact specifications within the day, it was already late afternoon and he'd driven for hours and made close to thirty phone calls.

The ring, however, pulsed and throbbed in its little velvet-lined box in the inside pocket of his jacket.

He'd obtained Fiona's ring size last night while she was sleeping, using one of her own shed hairs to very carefully measure and record the size of her ring finger. The element of secrecy and wondering how he'd explain himself if she woke up gave the whole endeavor an air of adventure and mystery.

Would she be surprised by a proposal? Of course. And there was always the possibility that she'd say no.

He didn't think she would, though. Was he being arrogant? Perhaps. Or simply realistic about the inability of most women, even extraordinary women, to say no to an estate the size of a small country and a large fortune accessible in any liquid currency. Fiona was a practical woman, and he felt sure he could convince her of the merits of marriage.

He also hoped he could do it before the all-important board meeting on Tuesday of next week.

A fire crackled in the grate of the great hall when he entered. Odd for this time of year.

"Afternoon, sir, let me take your coat." Lizzie, the housekeeper, approached. Then she whispered, "She said it was a bit chilly and asked to light the fire."

"Why not? I know it's still autumn and balmy for us, but compared to Singapore or California, it's downright freezing." He smiled. He liked that Fiona had felt free to make herself at home in the place that he hoped would soon be her home. At least for a few weekends a year.

Fiona stood at the sound of his voice. And smiled with what appeared to be genuine pleasure. A strange and unfamiliar sensation started to unfold in his chest. He realized that he was very glad to see her.

With a jolt he noticed his hand had wandered to the ring in his pocket, and he pulled it back to his side. He'd have to find the perfect moment for a proposal, when they were far away from the attentive ears of the staff. And when he could argue convincingly in his own favor without being heard. "Did you manage to keep busy today?"

"I did. I spent a few hours going through some of the rooms we looked into yesterday. I tried out each one of the candlesticks to see if they could possibly be a goblet stem in disguise."

"Any luck?"

"None whatsoever." She didn't look sad about that. "It could take a long time to find that cup fragment."

"If it even exists." Impatience zinged through him. Fiona looked even more beautiful than the girl who had fired his imagination as he drove like a demon on winding country roads all day. With her silky hair in a loose knot, and a fluffy white sweater over tight, dark jeans, she looked fresh and sexy, and his fingers itched to explore the textures and curves he'd grown acquainted with last night.

Will you marry me? He tested the question in his mind and tried to imagine her saying yes, but his imagination fell short when it came to putting words in her mouth. He'd have to wait.

They shared champagne and a walk in the garden before dinner. After they ate, he once again banished the staff, who must have known something was up, and they kissed and caressed, this time in the ladies' sitting room with its lush tapestries and a collection of watercolors by his more talented female ancestors.

He watched and waited for the right moment to reach for the ring, but never felt with conviction that the moment had arrived. He knew it would be like knowing the perfect price point to buy a rising stock, or the exact moment to go in for the kill in a meeting, and he was patient enough to wait.

They made love in his bed—frantic and breathless, then slow and sensual, exploring and enjoying each other's bodies. They giggled and held each other, and talked about all sorts of strange things he hadn't thought about in years: his first kiss (a girl at a dance arranged by his boarding school); his first great ambition (to play cricket for Scotland); how many children he hoped to have (three).

"Why three?" Her eyes shone with warmth and interest.

"I have no idea. I came up with that on the spot. I'm not sure I've ever thought about it before."

She hesitated for a moment. "And suddenly you are."

"Yes." The moment burned with promise. Was it

time to grab the ring from his jacket, which now lay crumpled on the floor somewhere? He didn't want to break up their perfect embrace. Her arms were wrapped around him like a pair of warm angel wings. "But now it's your turn. When was your first kiss?"

"I was seventeen, and felt like the last girl in my grade to be kissed. Danny Adams finally broke the curse in the parking lot behind the bowling alley."

"It sounds very romantic."

"I wish it was. His braces snagged in my hair when he tried to kiss my ear, and we never really made it back from that."

He laughed. "I can't picture you as a gawky teen."

"Please don't. It wasn't a pretty picture. I'm so much happier as a grown-up. And I'm totally over my first ambition of being an air force pilot."

He lifted a brow. "What happened?"

She grinned. "I don't like being told what to do, so I'm definitely better off being self-employed."

"And how many children?" His heart pumped almost audibly. He knew they were talking about their future, the one they'd share. He could feel it as easily as he could feel the heat from her skin warming his own.

"Hmm. I have two younger brothers, and I admit there were times when I wished I was an only child. But in retrospect I have to agree that three is a nice, round number. An heir and a spare and plenty of room for someone to be the black sheep." She grinned.

"See? I knew there was a good reason for me picking three. We agree on a lot of things." A warm silence, pregnant with possibilities, stretched between them. But it still wasn't the time. They were building toward it, step by step, as the pharaohs had built the pyramids. Better to take it slow and steady and make sure all the foundations were in place, than rush and miscalculate and show up in the boardroom next Tuesday with no momentous news to announce.

He wasn't at all sure the deal with SK Industries that he'd spent a year building would go through without his change of marital status. The chairman of the board had expressed his strong disapproval that a man of James's age and status had no family to speak of and went home alone each night. James might have ignored it if it wasn't the fifth or sixth time he'd heard the same thing—usually second- or third-hand—in the past year. And if he hadn't started, silently, to agree. "Three's a perfect number. Or even four if the last one is a set of twins." He stroked her cheek.

"Now I'm starting to feel tired." She smiled, resting her head on his chest. He couldn't believe how comfortable he felt with her, talking about things he'd never discussed with anyone. It only strengthened his conviction that Fiona was the one.

Now all he had to do was convince her of that.

Fiona woke in a dreamy state the next morning, one arm still draped across James's broad chest. What a night. James continued to surprise her. She tried to remind herself that she was one in a long line of women he'd seduced and bedded and was simply the latest victim of his charms. It was hard, though. If she didn't know better she'd almost think he really liked her.

They ate a leisurely breakfast together, then headed out for a ride. She rode the adorable Taffy again, and James rode a majestic dark bay called Solomon. They cantered across the green fields around the estate, slowing to a walk as they left the manicured swards of grass and ventured out into the rugged hills. Brown from a distance, up close the hills glittered with colorful heather, in lavenders and pinks and whites, bursting with life under the bright sky.

"This landscape is unbelievable." She looked at James, who rode along on a loose rein, looking every inch the dashing medieval prince. "How come it's not covered with tract homes, or shopping malls?"

He laughed. "Too remote. And the best thing about owning everything the eye can see is that you can control its future."

No doubt his modus operandi in the business world, as well.

"This mound dates back at least five thousand years." He steered his horse up a narrow track onto a swelling in the heather-clad terrain that rose about twenty feet above the surrounding plain.

"Why was it built?"

"We don't know. One of the many mysteries of this landscape." From the top you could look down into a green valley where a village hugged the banks of a river, a church steeple rising above the roofs. "I like to come up and think about all the people who've walked and ridden here before. It gives me a sense of perspective on my place in the universe."

"One more in a long line of people to walk this way." The thought gave her chills. She felt so small against the grand landscape.

"Exactly." He jumped down from his horse. "Let me help you dismount." Holding his reins in one hand, he approached her.

"Here?" Why would they get off out here in the middle of nowhere?

He nodded, a tiny smile tugging at his lips. Apprehension crept over her. A sense of something about to

OFFICIAL OPINION POLL

Dear Reader,

Since you are a book enthusiast, we would like to know what you think.

Inside you will find a short Opinion Poll. Please participate in our poll by sharing your opinion on 3 subjects that are very important to all of us.

To thank you for your participation, we would like to send you **2 FREE BOOKS** and **2 FREE GIFTS!**

Please enjoy them with our compliments.

Sincerely,

Pam Powers

YOUR OPINION POLL
THANK-YOU FREE GIFTS INCLUDE:

▶ **2 HARLEQUIN DESIRE® BOOKS**
▶ **2 LOVELY SURPRISE GIFTS**

OFFICIAL OPINION POLL

YOUR OPINION COUNTS!
Please check TRUE or FALSE below to express your opinion about the following statements:

Q1 Do you believe in "true love"?

"TRUE LOVE HAPPENS ONLY ONCE IN A LIFETIME."
○ TRUE
○ FALSE

Q2 Do you think marriage has any value in today's world?

"YOU CAN BE TOTALLY COMMITTED TO SOMEONE WITHOUT BEING MARRIED."
○ TRUE
○ FALSE

Q3 What kind of books do you enjoy?

"A GREAT NOVEL MUST HAVE A HAPPY ENDING."
○ TRUE
○ FALSE

YES! I have placed my sticker in the space provided below. Please send me the **2 FREE books** and **2 FREE gifts** for which I qualify. I understand that I am under no obligation to purchase anything further, as explained on the back of this card.

225/326 HDL FVPJ

FIRST NAME

LAST NAME

ADDRESS

APT.#

CITY

STATE/PROV.

ZIP/POSTAL CODE

HARLEQUIN® READER SERVICE—Here's How It Works:

Accepting your 2 free books and 2 free gifts (gifts valued at approximately $10.00) places you under no obligation to buy anything. You may keep the books and gifts and return the shipping statement marked "cancel." If you do not cancel, about a month later we'll send you 6 additional books and bill you just $4.30 each in the U.S. or $4.99 each in Canada. That is a savings of at least 14% off the cover price. It's quite a bargain! Shipping and handling is just 50¢ per book in the U.S. and 75¢ per book in Canada.* You may cancel at any time, but if you choose to continue, every month we'll send you 6 more books, which you may either purchase at the discount price or return to us and cancel your subscription.

*Terms and prices subject to change without notice. Prices do not include applicable taxes. Sales tax applicable in N.Y. Canadian residents will be charged applicable taxes. Offer not valid in Quebec. Books received may not be as shown. All orders subject to credit approval. Credit or debit balances in a customer's account(s) may be offset by any other outstanding balance owed by or to the customer. Please allow 4 to 6 weeks for delivery. Offer available while quantities last.

If offer card is missing write to: Harlequin Reader Service, P.O. Box 1867, Buffalo NY 14240-1867 or visit: www.ReaderService.com

BUSINESS REPLY MAIL
FIRST-CLASS MAIL   PERMIT NO. 717   BUFFALO, NY

POSTAGE WILL BE PAID BY ADDRESSEE

HARLEQUIN READER SERVICE
PO BOX 1341
BUFFALO NY 14240-8571

NO POSTAGE
NECESSARY
IF MAILED
IN THE
UNITED STATES

happen. She jumped down to the soft, mossy turf. Their horses were blowing with exertion, steam rising from their bodies in the relatively cool air.

James did something with the horses' reins that kept them knotted up around their neck, then left them standing together. Both just stood there, blinking and steaming, as he walked back to her. "Will they simply wait?"

"They're trained to, for hunting. Though you can never entirely tell what horses will do." He glanced back at them with a smile. As he approached her she saw him reach into one of the pockets of his dark green jacket, and an expression of concentration crossed his face.

Her breath came faster as he stopped right in front of her and reached for her hand. She gave it to him and hoped it wasn't sweating. Was he going to kiss her? Her lips tingled in anticipation.

"Fiona…" He paused for a moment and frowned. The intense look in his slate-gray eyes made her pulse ratchet higher. "Do you ever just know when something is right?"

"Um, sure." It was hard to think with him standing there holding her hand, with that piercing gaze fixed on her. And the two horses watching like spectators.

He held her one hand in both of his. "I pride myself on my instincts. They've stood me well over the years. And my instincts tell me that you're…different."

She swallowed. Had he realized she wasn't really there to help him find the cup? Had he sniffed out her true motive? Fear clawed at her heart.

But his gaze had softened. "I felt it the moment I met you. You're smart, and serious, and you chart your own course in life. I knew immediately you were someone I could talk to, and you'd understand."

She nodded, not sure what to say. This conversation

was so strange, with him holding her hand out here in the middle of nowhere. If she didn't know better she'd almost suspect he was about to propose marriage or something crazy like that.

As she had the thought he went down on one knee on the damp turf and reached into his pocket. Her jaw dropped as her heartbeat bumped up to maximum speed.

"Fiona, every instinct in my mind and body tells me that you're the woman for me. I know we've only known each other a short time, but I feel sure that we'd form a powerful and loving partnership that could take on the world." He drew in a steady breath. "Fiona, will you marry me?"

It was lucky he still held her hand or she might have fallen right over. Had she imagined the whole thing? It seemed too coincidental for her to suddenly think he might propose—out of the blue and for no good reason—then to have him actually do it.

"Uh…" Her brain was a tumbled mess of thoughts, none of them an appropriate answer. "I…I…" She didn't know what she thought, or what to say. *No* seemed an obvious answer, but a refusal would end their short relationship, and she didn't want to do that.

She didn't want to ruin her chances of making her father happy. And she also didn't want to say goodbye to James. She'd enjoyed their time together more than…more than anything she could remember. Fear and longing rose inside her. She wanted to spend more days galloping through the countryside with him, and more nights folded in his arms.

Blood thundered in her ears as he waited for her answer. "Yes, I will." The words burst from her mouth before she even decided to say them. Somewhere in her autonomic nervous system a button had been pressed and her future decided without the more complex workings of her ego being consulted.

"Fantastic!" A broad smile spread across James's face. He rose to his feet, whipped out a ring, a large sparkling diamond, and slid it onto her ring finger before she had time to catch her breath.

She blinked. The air around them suddenly seemed so bright and hot she could hardly see or breathe. Had she really just agreed to marry James Drummond?

Their lips met in a passionate kiss that was a huge relief because it meant she didn't have to come up with any words. His strong arms around her felt wonderful, but all the time her brain was racing. Why had he proposed? What made him think she'd say yes? His arrogance was extraordinary.

Yet she had said yes.

They pulled apart, and she found herself staring at his face. The chiseled, eye-catchingly handsome face of a man descended from warriors, with more land and money than some small nations. And he wanted to be her husband.

"You look rather shell-shocked."

"That's because I am." It was a relief to admit it. They weren't actually going to get married, of course. In between now and the imaginary wedding she'd just agreed to, their relationship would somehow fizzle out and they'd go their separate ways. It was a temporary fantasy they'd both agreed to participate in. "In a good way."

"I'm glad you could see that although we haven't known each other long, there's no reason for delay. You're decisive. I think it's the same instinct that makes us so successful in business."

"Yes." She agreed blindly, still incapable of actual thought. "Absolutely."

"We'll get married right away. We're not kids who need a long engagement. We can probably do it next week."

Fiona's throat tightened. "But…my parents." She thought immediately of her dad, who would probably have a stroke if she actually married James Drummond. But her mom and stepdad would be devastated if she got married without them present. Not that she was really getting married. "And we should spend more time getting to know each other."

"Of course we'll include them. I know just the planner to organize an event everyone will remember."

He held both her hands, and they were definitely sweating. "I need time to…find the right dress." Her brain scrambled for roadblocks to slow down this freight train that seemed to be getting out of control. "And my bridesmaids and maid of honor." All things she'd never given a moment's thought to.

James's brow rose, and humor twinkled in his eyes. "Do you really want those trappings of tradition?"

"Oh, yes." It was hard to speak with her heart thumping against her ribs like a caged animal.

"Then you shall have them." A smile lit up his face and toasted her heart with its warmth. James Drummond wanted to marry her. It didn't get any stranger than this. Why did he have to be so handsome and intelligent and, well, awesome? She'd never in a million years have dreamed that someone like this would want to marry her. She wasn't a jaw-dropping beauty or a brilliant conversationalist. Even now that she was wealthy, men were hardly stopping her in the street to invite her out. And this man, undoubtedly one of the world's most eligible bachelors, wanted to rush her to the altar. It didn't make sense. He must have some ulterior motive. But what?

Taffy had grown tired of standing still and was trying to stretch her neck down to nibble the heather. "We should probably..." What? The words fizzled.

"Of course." James strode toward the horses and untied their reins, then handed her Taffy's. She climbed onto the horse with a sense of relief. She'd probably never needed a good gallop more in her life. The ring twinkled on her finger like an alien life form. She hoped it wouldn't fall off and get lost in the heather.

James beamed with apparent happiness. If she weren't so freaked out she'd be touched by it. Had he fallen madly in love with her? It didn't seem possible in such a short time, but she knew several people whose romances had been that sudden and dramatic. Supposedly true love was like that.

Of course that wasn't the feeling pumping in her heart. More like sheer terror and confusion tangled up with unexpected lust and passion. This man was something else.

They rode through a stretch of hilly country, and she had to concentrate to help Taffy down the winding and narrow trail. At the bottom was a nearly flat stretch of open grazing land. James looked at her. "Shall we?"

She knew exactly what he meant, and she nodded her reply. Together they set out across the grass, letting their horses build steam and stretch out their powerful necks and long legs, until they were both neck and neck in a flat-out gallop.

If there was a rabbit hole hidden in the grass, a horse could catch its leg and either of them could die in an instant. But the ground swept beneath them, firm and steady, and the air whipped her face, as if it might slap some sense into her. She knew she was grinning from ear to ear as they exploded through the open country like jockeys on a racetrack.

They slowed as they approached the estate, walking their sweating horses through a crowd of fluffy sheep. It was only then that Fiona realized they hadn't kissed after his proposal. It wasn't really romantic at all, almost a business proposition.

She sneaked a glance at James, who glowed with good cheer. Which made a twinge of unease uncurl in her belly. Could he be so happy thinking that they would get married? Or was this a practical arrangement for him in the same way it was for her.

"I don't think I've ridden that fast in years, if ever." James patted his horse's neck.

"Obviously you've been riding with the wrong people." She couldn't help smiling. His enthusiasm was infectious. "Though I'm pretty sure that was the best ride of my life."

"We'll have to make a habit of it, though there were moments when I started to think we were racing each other."

"Oh, no. If we were racing I'd have won." She lifted a brow. Taffy's broad back rose and fell underneath her, and at that moment anything seemed possible.

"That sounds like a challenge." James's eyes glittered with amusement.

"Most definitely." Then a thought occurred to her. A race, with a prize of her choosing. Not some tarnished piece of an old cup but something she really wanted. Her dad's factory. "In fact, I'm throwing down the gauntlet."

"You want to race me?"

"Not right this minute. I think our horses have had

enough for one day, but on a date to be determined, each of us on horses of our own choosing, yes. I'd like to race you."

He rode along staring at her, hips shifting with the movement of his horse's back. "You're on."

"What does the winner get as a prize?" Her heart beat faster as she hoped for the opening she needed.

"Hmm, that's a tough one, since I suspect we both have everything we want." He stared at the gray walls of the estate.

"I'm looking for property in Singapore, and you own some. How about if I get to choose one of your properties if I win?" Terror soared in her chest as she laid out her plan. If he said no, it would be harder to come back and try again. He might get suspicious.

"A property in Singapore." He frowned. "That sounds doable. But what do I get if I win? Or should I say, *when* I win." His arrogance should have annoyed her, but at that minute she was too thrilled that her crazy plan might actually work.

But what could she offer him? She was pretty sure he wouldn't win. He probably weighed nearly twice what she did, and there was a reason jockeys were chosen for their light weight. Also, he clearly wasn't used to getting up off his horse's back into two-point, whereas she found it easy. In a fair race, on evenly matched horses, she knew she would win. "How about six months of my time working on any project of your choice?"

"As a consultant?"

"Yes."

"I suppose that would be convenient for both of us since we'll be married and living under the same roof."

She froze. Which wasn't easy since Taffy still moved underneath her. She hadn't factored the whole marriage thing into her wager. How would she work with him for six months and manage to break off this crazy engagement that made no sense?

That wouldn't be necessary, though. He wouldn't win. She'd win and get her dad's factory back, then take off for California and safety—emotional and otherwise.

"Yes. I'd be able to work on your project twenty-four hours a day." She hated herself. First for agreeing to marry a man she barely knew, and had no intention of wedding, second for fibbing about promising to work for him. Trying to win her dad's affection was taking a much larger emotional toll than she'd expected. For the first time it occurred to her that this plan was flawed from the get-go.

On the other hand she was in too deep to stop now.

He rode right up next to her and extended his hand. "You're on."

She shook it. She'd never go back on a handshake deal. Whatever happened she'd stick by this part of their arrangement, even if it meant working for a man who by then hated her.

She'd just have to make sure that didn't happen.

Seven

Dinner was served with champagne. "To our future." James raised his glass and she met it with hers.

She smiled and hoped it wasn't too shaky. "I admit I'm a little worried about the curse of doom hanging over the Drummonds. We haven't made any headway toward finding that cup piece." She cut into her roasted salmon.

"I'd almost forgotten about that."

"It's the whole reason you brought me here."

"Not the whole reason."

"You knew you were going to propose to me?"

"Let's just say I had some ideas in that direction." He sipped his champagne with a somewhat predatory gaze.

"But you didn't even know me."

"I'm a big believer in gut instinct. I can size up a stock chart, or a start-up company or even a person in a glance. I don't always act on my gut, but when I do I'm usually right."

"And your gut was telling you good things about me."

"Very good things." He took a bite of salmon.

Her tiny new potatoes looked huge, and the green beans threatened to lodge in her throat. Guilt must be killing her appetite. James had no idea how far off course his gut instinct had led him this time. Still, it was so arrogant of him to be already planning their engagement when they'd barely met that he probably deserved it.

"I think the wedding should take place mid next month. It's usually a pretty quiet time on the business front, so we can take some time for a honeymoon. Where have you always wanted to go?"

A honeymoon! She blinked and sipped at her champagne while she tried to gather her thoughts. "Next month is so soon. It'll take time to find the perfect dress."

"It'll be easy. You simply choose a good designer and tell them what you want. Takes all the drama out of shopping. I can recommend an excellent tailor in Singapore."

She inhaled carefully. "My family may need some time to get used to the idea."

"Why? You're hardly a child bride." Then he hesitated and frowned. "Do you think they won't like me for some reason?"

His sudden concern touched her. If he only knew. "I'm sure they'd love you once they get to know you, but you know how people don't like surprises. They'll need to warm up to you a bit."

"We'll fly them in next week. Your mom can help

you organize the dress and any of that other wedding stuff you want to do."

She swallowed. She couldn't even imagine how her mom and stepdad in California would react, but her dad in Singapore was bound to blow his top. "When are we going to have our race?"

"Race?"

"You know, the horse race. Whoever wins…" Her voice trailed off. She knew she'd brought it up at the wrong moment, but it seemed the only escape route from this freight train heading down a steep hillside with no brakes.

"We can do that when we get back from Singapore. In fact, I'd like to leave tomorrow." He pulled out his iPhone. "I'll text my pilot."

But… But… But. She couldn't even come up with anything. This was his house and if he wanted to leave it and go somewhere else, she could hardly disagree. Which was more than a little weird, if they were supposedly getting married. As his wife, or even his fiancée, she should be able to tell him she preferred to stay in Scotland, or that she had plans of her own. But their relationship wasn't on that kind of footing at all.

It wasn't a relationship of equals. He had something she needed, and she was skulking around trying to get it. Obviously, he needed something, too—marriage to her. She couldn't figure out his reasons. He seemed to genuinely like her, but that wasn't enough. Not for this kind of rush. But she couldn't ask about his motives, because then he might ask about hers.

He looked up from his phone after about a minute. "We'll leave here at 6:00 a.m."

"Lucky thing I never finished unpacking. Are we simply abandoning the search for the cup?"

"I think we're quite lucky enough without it."

She took a swallow of champagne, and it burned her throat. "Yes, I suppose we are."

They slept together in James's bed. She took the big engagement ring off and left it on the dresser. It felt like taking off a ball and chain. When they were naked, under the sheets, skin to skin, somehow she could forget all the complications of their crazy engagement and all her schemes and underhanded motives.

His kisses sent delicious ripples of pleasure coursing through her. His hands, so assured and yet so tender, made her skin hum. She loved to touch his body. His competitive instincts kept him active in several sports, and the results were impressive.

And he seemed to enjoy her body every bit as much as she reveled in his. He licked and kissed delicate patterns on her skin, making her gasp when he hit on an erogenous zone. Slow and deliberate, he visited each part of her body with his mouth, and left it throbbing and pulsing with desire. No *wham bam, thank you ma'am* for James Drummond. He played her body like a fine instrument, finding the high notes and making it vibrate with sensations she'd never known before.

She found herself eagerly returning the favor. His subtle, masculine scent filled her senses, and she enjoyed the roughness of his skin. Her tongue and teeth trailed over the firm contours of his powerful chest, and along the fine trail of dark hair to his proud erection.

She was almost ready to explode with anticipation when she finally climbed on top of him and took him very slowly inside her. James groaned, and she enjoyed the intense expression that crossed his face as she took him deep. Why did he have to be so handsome? She'd never kissed a man this beautiful, let alone been engaged to one. Even under the rather awkward circumstances, it was enough to make a girl lose her head.

So she let her tiresome, worried thoughts float away and hang out somewhere near the vaulted ceiling, while the rest of her enjoyed making love to James.

He was a patient lover, and endlessly creative. He found positions she'd never imagined that made her toes curl with unexpected pleasure. Every time she thought she'd reached the point of no return, he'd pull her carefully back and begin the dance of driving her wild with excitement all over again. It was like riding a roller coaster, except far more unpredictable and pleasurable.

Kind of like her life right now.

She made some strange sounds when she finally arrived at her long-awaited orgasm. She heard them from very far away. James had gathered her up and taken her into a distant realm where nothing mattered except the present moment and the fierce passion they shared.

Afterward they lay in each other's arms. She felt utterly relaxed and at peace, which didn't make any sense at all, but that didn't seem to matter.

He's amazing. James was so kind and thoughtful, so obviously brilliant, sexy, gorgeous. And for some strange reason he wanted to marry her, Fiona Lam.

Too weird. Weird and wonderful if it wasn't for the awkward family entanglement that had brought her face-to-face with him in the first place. Her plans had already gone so far off course it was impossible to know where she would end up. Maybe right here in James's arms?

At this moment anything seemed possible.

She told her mom she had "met someone" and wanted them to meet him. Her mom was thrilled at the chance to visit Singapore, and peppered her with questions about James. James insisted on paying for everything, so all her mom and stepdad had to do was book the tickets. Since they were both from Singapore originally, they had loads of friends and family to visit and couldn't wait.

Fiona somehow neglected to mention that she was getting married. Because she wasn't getting married.

Or was she? The announcement James had prepared for release to the *Straits Times* stated that she and James Farquahar Drummond, Twelfth Earl of Ballantrae, were engaged. She'd told him not to send it until she had a chance to break the news to them. She didn't tell him it contained glaring errors. The announcement included her stepdad's name, which was Lam, like hers. Her mom had changed Fiona's surname when they moved to California and became hysterical if Fiona ever talked about changing it back. Maybe that was another reason why she felt the need to try to make so much up to her father.

But unless James had hired a private detective—which he apparently hadn't—he and everyone else thought her stepdad was her real father.

In the best room at the Four Seasons, at James's insistence, her mom pulled clothes from her extensive luggage, while her stepdad experimented with the TV remote.

"Really, sweetheart, we could have stayed with my sister. I don't know why I brought this dress. It's far too hot here. I forgot how hot it is. And I still don't understand why we had to come here in such a rush."

To help me choose my wedding dress. Or not. "I wanted you to meet my new…boyfriend." She couldn't bring herself to say *fiancé* to her own mother, when she had no intention of marrying him.

"You two must be serious." Her mom paused, a satin negligee in hand. A broad smile broke out on her face. "I'm so happy that you're dating. You never seem interested in boys."

"He's not really a boy." She couldn't help smiling. "He's several years older than me."

Her mom waved a hand. "That's nothing. A husband should be older than his wife. And he's Singaporean! I can't believe I moved across the world and my daughter goes back home to find a husband."

"Actually, he's Scottish." Even though she was telling the absolute truth, this whole conversation felt like a horrible wasp's nest of lies she was building. "He does a lot of business here. I visited him in Scotland, though. He has a big castle out in the middle of nowhere."

"A castle?" Her mom almost dropped the shirt she was putting on a hanger. "Dan, did you hear that? A castle!"

Fiona nodded. It was hard not to smile. Wouldn't it be fabulous if she and James really were madly in love and getting married? It would be like some kind of fairy tale come true.

But fairy tales didn't come true. Not in her life, anyway. She wondered what her mom would think if she knew her whole relationship was phony. She certainly wouldn't find it entertaining the way her dad did. He'd chuckled and promised to keep quiet when the engagement was announced. Her mom was a gentle person whose main goal in life was to make others happy. She hadn't been able to make Fiona's dad happy, and she'd warned Fiona about expecting too much from him. Fiona didn't worry, though. She and her dad were a lot more alike than her mom gave her credit for.

"So when do I meet this amazing man?"

"At dinner tonight." Her stomach constricted. James had booked them a table at the most impossible-to-get-into restaurant in town. Where he was no doubt going to start conversations about wedding dresses and engagement parties and guest lists. She doubted the topic of her real dad would come up, since her mom tended to act as if he'd never existed and her stepdad, Dan, was her birth father. Still, a situation like this could explode in her face. "But maybe we should cancel. You're probably tired."

"Nonsense. I can't wait!"

An hour later she met James at his penthouse apartment. Her heart jumped as he opened the door, and her lips tingled in anticipation of their kiss.

Which was rich and full and made her toes curl.

Why did he have to be so delicious? He looked devastating in a dark suit—apparently this man never wore jeans—with his hair slicked back and slightly damp. "I've missed you." His low murmur stirred the desire already rising inside her.

"I've missed you, too." Worse yet, it was true. She'd both dreaded and longed to see him in equal measure.

"We have an hour and a half before our reservation. Shall we go pick up your parents and take them out for a drink?"

"No." She said it too fast. "I mean, they're resting after their flight. They'll meet us at the restaurant. They're both from Singapore so they know their way around."

"Perfect." He smiled. "Won't you come in?"

She glanced over his shoulder into the sleek, minimalist interior. "How about a walk?" She didn't really want to come in and kiss him and get all hot and confused. Better to stick to her goals and try to keep this thing on track. And her dad's factory was only about five blocks away. "I'd love some air and a chance to stretch my legs. I'm nervous about you meeting my parents."

Truer words were never spoken.

"Don't be nervous. I'm quite well behaved." His mischievous grin was adorable. "And I promise to charm them."

"I'm sure you will."

He slipped his arm through hers, which sent a shiver of excitement right through her. How odd that they'd slept together in Scotland, but back here he seemed to want them to stay apart. Really, it was better, but she couldn't help feeling slightly hurt. Which was ridiculous. "Uh, I haven't yet told my parents we're getting married."

"Why not?"

"I want them to meet you and like you before I tell them."

"Sounds like a sensible plan." His beaming smile made her feel so guilty. Especially as their stroll took them out of the expensive shopping district toward the more up-and-coming area where the factory lay. She knew exactly which building it was, but James had no idea she'd ever heard of it before. She slowed the pace as they drew near. The concrete shoebox looked even more depressing than she remembered, with Chinese characters daubed in green paint directly onto its mildewed surface. Old window air conditioners provided nesting for local birds, and there was garbage sitting on the front doorstep. How did you tactfully express an interest in a dump like this?

"You're not going to believe it, but I just bought this

building." James took the weight off by bringing it up himself.

"Why? It looks like a wreck." She worked hard not to show her excitement.

"The land under it, of course. Some old guy had been sitting on it, operating some kind of factory at a near loss for years. Since taxes are based on the potential value of the land—as if it had a new multi-unit building—he didn't make enough to pay them. So I stepped in, paid them and now it's mine." He gazed proudly at his ugly new acquisition.

"That seems rather unfair." She wanted to see how James felt about this. "Why can't they tax it as it is right now?"

"It's to prevent people squatting on promising pieces of real estate. If half the waterfront were lined with fishermen's shacks, Singapore wouldn't be the great city it is today. And, of course, it brings in revenue that pays for services."

"But what about the poor guy who lost his building?" Why was she treading into such dangerous territory? She must be mad. But she couldn't seem to help herself.

"It's business. If he wanted to make money he could have developed the property himself. Maybe he was planning to, but if you're going to do that, you have to pay the taxes. I keep my eyes open for opportunities like this all the time. I've gained some of my best properties this way."

"What are you going to build here?"

"I haven't decided yet. At first I thought a small office complex would be good. There are a lot of companies out there that need more space. But since the retail area has expanded in this direction, now I'm thinking it could be a destination retail space."

"Like the one I plan to build."

"Exactly."

A chill rose through her as she realized she'd accomplished exactly what she needed to do. The groundwork was set. And she was every bit as devious, coldhearted and ruthless as any business tycoon in Singapore.

She quickened the pace, wanting to leave before there was any further discussion of "the old guy" who owned the place. James's arm was still linked with hers, and she tried not to think about the muscle moving beneath his expensive suit. Better to think of him as a business entity, not a man with feelings and emotions. She knew he must have his reasons for their sudden engagement, and sooner or later she'd find out what they were and feel better about her deception. "Maybe we should head for the restaurant."

James glowed with pleasure as he ordered wine for their party. Fiona's mother was charming and gregarious and her husband soft-spoken and funny. Even though the stakes were high he felt quite at ease. Fiona was rather quiet, but perhaps she was overwhelmed by so much happening so quickly. Who wouldn't be?

"So you only met two weeks ago?" Fiona's mom seemed to want all the details. Which were rather thin and made him uncomfortable when she shone the bright light of curiosity on them. He could understand why Fiona wanted them to get to know him before she announced their impending marriage. Still, they had to get past the preliminaries and get everyone on the same page, as he'd already made arrangements for their engagement party the following week in the ballroom at the Marina Bay Sands hotel.

"We've traveled a long way in two weeks." He rested his hand on Fiona's. It felt oddly tense.

"Literally and figuratively." Her smile was oddly bright. "Scotland and back!"

"Fiona tells me you have a castle." Her mom leaned in and peered at him through her glasses. "Did you build it yourself?"

He laughed. "God, no. I'd have made it a lot smaller and better insulated. The oldest parts of the castle date back to Roman times. Every now and then someone tries to make improvements, but they don't help much. Fiona tells me you're from Singapore."

"Yes, lah! Didn't leave the place until I was twenty-six and met Dan." She patted her husband's arm affectionately. "And he spirited me off to California when he got transferred there by his bank."

Relieved that he'd managed to steer the conversation off him and Fiona briefly, he asked her questions about Singapore and what had changed. As Dan regaled them with a story about his grandmother who owned a noodle shop, James saw the man he'd been waiting for enter the restaurant. "Do excuse me." He rose from the table and walked past several white-clothed tables of elegantly dressed diners, before extending his hand to Goh Kwon Beng, the president and CEO of SK Industries and the man whose partnership could remove nearly every obstacle from his most ambitious project ever. "What a surprise." He knew Beng dined there at least three times a week with his wife and daughters, who had headed off to their usual table, so their encounter was anything but accidental. "I'm here entertaining my fiancée's parents." He gestured to the table, where Fiona and her mom and stepdad were conveniently laughing about something.

Beng frowned and peered at the group. "I didn't know you were engaged."

"It's not been formally announced yet, but we'll be celebrating next weekend. I do hope you'll be able to attend." Fiona had insisted on telling her parents in person before releasing the engagement announcement to the papers.

Beng seized him with both hands. "Congratulations! And welcome to the world of men. You'll appreciate how much easier and more content your life will be once you have a wife."

"It was a long journey to find the right woman, but happily I've arrived. Would you like to meet them?"

"I'd be delighted."

James realized on the way to the table that he'd just announced his impending marriage, when his in-laws knew nothing about it. This would take some deft handling. "Fiona, this is Goh Kwon Beng, one of my wisest and sharpest business associates. And this is Fiona Lam." Before Beng could get a word in edgeways— congratulations, for example—he introduced her mother and father and rattled off a long itinerary of all the things they should catch up on while they were in Singapore after a long absence. This led to an exchange about the old days, and the noodle shop on Penang Road and some laughter before one of Beng's daughters came over to retrieve him so they could order.

James sank into his chair with relief as Beng retreated.

Fiona's mother smiled. "What a nice man! He looks familiar. I feel like I've seen his face before."

"He's the head of SK Industries." Fiona watched the retreating Beng. "One of the most powerful men in Singapore." She shot a glance at James, which chilled him slightly. Did she know what he was up to, or have any suspicions? She was probably too smart not to. Part of him couldn't believe she'd agreed to marry him so easily. Then again, there was a real connection between them and she must be able to feel it, too. "You have friends in high places, James." The sparkle in her eyes relieved him. She seemed impressed rather than suspicious. Maybe she would like to discuss her retail project with Beng. His vast distribution network had a finger in almost every retail pie in the region. He slid his arm around her for a moment, wanting to feel the warmth of her body and reassure her—or reassure himself?—of the deeper connection between them.

Dinner was delicious, and the conversation flowed as fast as the wine. By the end of the four-course meal they were all laughing.

"James, I can see why Fiona's fallen for you so fast. I must commend her on her excellent taste." Her mom squeezed her hand. Fiona looked a little tense, but smiled back. "Love often happens fast, and when you least expect it. I have a funny feeling that soon you'll be planning your wedding."

James glanced at Fiona—now was the perfect moment to share their news. But Fiona stared straight ahead with a forced bright look on her face and laughed. "You might well be right!"

He stiffened. Why didn't she want to tell them yet? But he told himself to hold back. It was all happening very fast and she might need more time to adjust. It was hard to be patient, though. He had deadlines involving his negotiations with SK Industries, and a big wedding would play very nicely into those. Gathering all the local rainmakers together with champagne and cake and visions of his new patriarchal image was the finishing touch he needed for five or six different deals he had in mind. But he knew from long experience that some deals couldn't be rushed.

After dinner his plans to spend the night with Fiona were scuppered when she insisted on taking her parents back to their hotel. All he got was a rushed, "I'll call you later." But she didn't call.

At eleven o'clock James grew impatient and phoned her. "I miss you."

"I miss you, too." There was an odd tightness to her voice.

"I don't know where you live."

Again, the laugh that shriveled intimacy. "I think it's better that way."

"I need to see you, tonight. I can have my driver come pick you up." The driver wouldn't be too thrilled by his late-night assignment, but he was paid handsomely enough. And though he didn't want to ruin his new traditional family man image by being spotted cavorting with his future wife before marriage, how many people were likely to see her coming up to his apartment near midnight?

"I think I should get some sleep. I'm exhausted after today."

The sharp pang of disappointment surprised him. He'd spent the evening with this woman. Why did her absence hurt him already? "You could come sleep in my arms." He craved the feel of her soft cheek against his chest. He wanted to wake with her and see the sparkle in her eyes outshine the sun.

Clearly, he was losing it. "Please."

"I'd love to, James, but it's not a good idea. Let's have lunch tomorrow." The bright tone in her voice clashed in his ears like cymbals. Lunch, no doubt in a public place where he couldn't take her in his arms and kiss her as if the world was ending.

"How about lunch at my place?"

"Uh, okay."

Her hesitation hurt him. Which was insane! Why was he pining over this woman like a puppy? She'd already agreed to marry him. He needed to get himself together. "Twelve noon. I'll have my driver pick you up. What's your address?"

"I'm not sure where I'll be. I'll come to your place."

James hung up the phone with an odd sense of foreboding. He didn't feel entirely in control of this situation, and that was a very uncomfortable sensation for him. Tonight he was going to find out where she lived.

Eight

Adrenaline surged through Fiona three days later as she knocked on the scarred door to her dad's tiny apartment. She'd offered to buy him a house, but he wouldn't hear of it. Far too proud.

"Eh?" His gruff voice from inside made her chest constrict.

"It's me. Fiona."

The door swung open, releasing a cloud of cigarette smoke. She squinted and managed not to cough. "I don't like you coming here. It's a dump. I'd never live here if it wasn't for that devil who ruined me." He looked tired and older than the last time she'd seen him. A pang of affection rocked her. She wanted so badly to turn his life around so they could simply enjoy the simple pleasures together without any lingering bitterness.

"Have you seen the papers?" She wasn't sure if he'd

read the engagement announcement. So far he'd been good about keeping quiet.

"What papers? I don't read that garbage."

"Can I come in?" She didn't want to blurt her business out on the street. Thank heaven her mom and stepfather were busy visiting old friends today.

"The place is a mess. Let's go out. I'm buying." He grabbed a few crumpled bills out of a drawer.

"Nonsense. It's my treat. I have something to celebrate."

"Oh, yes?" He looked at her intently.

"Well, I will soon. I've figured out how to get your factory back." She spoke in hushed tones as he closed the door and they set out for the restaurant.

"By marrying James Drummond." His brows lowered.

He had heard. "It's not what you think, Dad. It's part of my plan."

"You'll get my revenge by making his life a misery?"

"No! I have a thing set up. A horse race. When I win it he has to give me whatever I want, and I'm going to ask for your factory." They hurried along the street toward the restaurant she had in mind. Their route would take them right past the factory.

Her father stared, his eyes slightly bloodshot. "A horse race?"

"I rode with him on the estate. Fast. I know I can beat him as I'm so much lighter. Don't worry about it."

"And he'll give you the factory? You actually discussed this."

"We haven't gone into detail. I don't want to make him suspicious."

"Maybe you should ask for his new tower down by

the park. That's worth a lot more than that old factory."
He chuckled. This idea obviously appealed to him.

"Let's keep it simple." She drew in a breath. "And
in the meantime I have to play along with this engagement charade. Last night was interesting since he took
Mom and Dan out to dinner."

Her dad's stride missed a beat. "She's here? What's
going on?"

Like most kids, she'd once dreamed of her parents
getting back together, but those fantasies were long
gone. "James wanted to meet her and tell her about
the engagement. I managed to hold him off from that,
though. Unfortunately, she really liked him."

"Slimy bastard. I bet he's a real charmer."

"He is." She felt a rogue urge to defend James and
point out that he had been kind to her. But she knew
that was a bad idea. "I have to go to some parties and
smile for a week or so, then we'll return to Scotland
and I'll win the race."

"You're more devious than he is." Her dad ran a
hand through his thinning hair. "It's a crazy scheme
and I like it!"

He stopped walking and hugged her. Her breath
caught in her lungs. It was the first time in her whole
life—that she could remember—that her dad had actually hugged her!

Tears welled up in her eyes and she hugged him back
as hard as she could. Which started him coughing. He
pulled back and reached for his cigarettes.

"You really should quit those," she said gently.

"I know. It's the stress. When you get me my factory back. Or that tower…" He burst into a coughing/
laughing fit, and she had to join in just to release all
the pent-up emotion.

When they approached the street with the factory on it, she grew nervous. The stakes were so high. What if she screwed up and lost the race and disappointed him? "There it is."

"What a dump. But the land is worth a fortune."

"That's why James bought it. What were you planning to do with the land?"

"A hotel. Or a shopping mall. I had several business partners interested."

"I could be your business partner." She could even launch the store she'd discussed with James. And this would be a chance to work closely with her dad every day! "We could work on the idea together."

He looked at her with surprise, and not a little suspicion.

"But only if you wanted to, Dad. I don't want to meddle in your business."

He laughed and coughed again. "You've turned into quite a firecracker, Fifi. You've got a lot of your grandmother in you."

"Your mom? I never met her. What was she like?"

They enjoyed a luxurious lunch at an outdoor restaurant with a view of the water. He told her stories of family members she never knew existed, opening up a whole history for her that gave her insight into both her dad and herself.

After a couple of drinks, and a large serving of steak, he seemed transformed back into the confident tycoon of her earliest childhood memories before her parents split up. Soon he'd be brandishing crisp banknotes and Cuban cigars and ordering drinks for his friends, the way she remembered from her childhood. It thrilled her that she could play a role in getting her dad back on his feet.

But every time she thought about James, she got a sharp pang of guilt. Would he be hurt? Probably not. She knew he didn't love her. He hadn't even pretended to. After last night's little introduction to Singapore's Mr. Big, she was pretty sure that marriage to her was simply a part of James's plan to ingratiate himself with the local magnates. She wasn't entirely sure why she fit the bill, but James must have thought it through and liked her credentials for some reason.

She didn't delude herself into thinking he actually cared. When she broke up with him he wouldn't be crushed and heartbroken; he'd merely be disappointed that a promising deal had fallen through. He'd find someone more congenial and probably be engaged again within weeks. There was certainly no shortage of women interested in marrying James Drummond.

As for herself, on the other hand…she wasn't at all sure how she'd feel in the aftermath of this whole mess. Her heart already felt as if it had been though a meat grinder.

She couldn't bear to go to James's apartment last night, though part of her had ached to. They'd have had more of that frighteningly hot sex, which was coming dangerously close to its familiar promise of "making love." Every time James kissed her she became further entangled in emotions she couldn't control. The devastating mix of chemical attraction and James's solicitous and tender affections was capable of bringing almost any woman to her knees. She'd thought she was strong, but she was getting nervous. She was in danger of genuinely falling for him. She needed to keep her emotions—and her body—locked up and as far from James as possible until this whole charade was played out.

* * *

Staying away from James didn't prove to be difficult. He was very busy with some deal he was making. Far from trying to keep him at arm's length, she found herself wondering why he hadn't called. Apparently, he thought he had her locked up, negotiations completed, and now he could set her quietly aside until he was ready to close the deal. The only way she knew he was even interested was that he sent her a huge bouquet of flowers every morning.

Which was more than a little alarming, since she'd never given him her address. He must have researched it, which meant he could have researched her background, too. Apparently, he hadn't found out anything that worried him, as his emails contained no probing questions. They were sweet and romantic, but didn't feel entirely genuine. Perhaps his secretary wrote them. Or maybe she was just trying to feel less guilty about her role in this whole marriage charade.

Then she got a hand-couriered envelope containing a stack of engraved invitations to their engagement party. They'd discussed the dates in passing and she'd been noncommittal. Apparently, James took that as her ready assent to any date he chose. The date was only five days away, at the most expensive venue in Singapore. His handwritten note invited her to send out as many as she wanted.

Uh-oh. This train was rolling faster down the hill. She hadn't said anything about their marriage plans to her mom, but obviously her parents would be expected at the party so she'd have to concoct something.

"I know we're engaged, but we won't get married for ages, Mom." They were rifling through racks of bridal gowns at an emporium full of extravagant designer dresses. Fiona hoped she wouldn't break out in hives. She wasn't cut out for these fluffy creations, and likely not for marriage, either. Her mom had insisted on coming here today since she was in town right now and might not get another chance to help her only daughter pick a dress for the biggest day in her life.

"Good. It's important to get to know someone first. I'd never have married your father if someone had given me that advice."

Stung, Fiona lifted her chin. "Then I wouldn't be here."

"I know, sweetheart." Her mom stroked her cheek. Which made her feel like a sulky teenager. "So in a way it all worked out for the best. But I want you to have a happy marriage."

"Didn't you like James?" Now that she was mad, she couldn't resist.

"He seems wonderful." She heard the edge of doubt in her mom's voice.

"But?"

"I don't know." She frowned. "Too wonderful, almost. So tall, handsome, charming…rich." Her mom smiled. "A little too good to be true."

"You don't think I'm good enough for someone like James?" Now she was getting ticked off!

"Of course you are, my love. I just see you with someone more…normal."

Me, too. This whole thing did seem like a crazy off-kilter fairy tale. Sooner or later the witch would show up and start throwing curses around. Or maybe she was the witch. "Well, anyway. I need to find something to wear for the engagement party. But like I said, I won't be getting married for a long time, so we can move away from this rack of white taffeta."

She noticed how she'd said, "I won't be getting married soon." Not *we*. She crossed the floor of the showroom to a rack of somber dresses. "Is it wrong to wear black for an engagement party?"

James picked her up for the party. She hadn't seen him in five days, so at least she hadn't had the terrible temptation of looking into those slate-gray eyes shining with desire.

Until now.

She climbed into the back of his car with him. He always used a driver in Singapore. He looked frighteningly handsome in a dark suit and a dark blue tie, and she'd forgotten how appealing his smile could be.

Their kiss sent jolts of energy rocketing to her fingers and toes. "I've missed you." She spoke the truth. Guilt and angst didn't prevent her from wanting to be with him.

"I've missed you more. I've kept busy, though. Our wedding plans are well under way. And there's a whole month for you to get ready." He smiled.

Fiona tried not to freak out. A month was a long time. They could easily have their race and deal with the aftermath with plenty of time to cancel a wedding that was an entire four weeks away. She realized she was chewing her lip. How twisted did she have to be to think about how to cancel her wedding while on the way to her own engagement party?

The driver dropped them off in front of the hotel, where arriving guests rushed up to James to greet him and congratulate them both on their happy news. Fiona's eyes bulged as they entered the grand ballroom, arm in arm. At least two hundred guests stood among the potted palms, sipping champagne, and they clapped when she and James entered. She tried to keep a smile plastered on her face while she greeted scores of people she'd never seen before.

A very tall blonde woman turned out to be James's mother—she'd quite forgotten he had one. Her name was Inez and she spoke with a central European accent, which took Fiona by surprise. She'd assumed that she was Scottish, or at least English. Suddenly, James's choice of a foreign bride didn't seem quite so offbeat. She greeted Fiona with a kiss on the cheek and said she hoped they'd be very happy together. Fiona had no idea what to say, so she babbled on about how much she loved the Scottish estate. James's mom got a look on her face that said *better you than me.* She got a sneaking feeling they wouldn't be seeing too much of each other, until she remembered that they definitely wouldn't be, because she and James weren't getting married.

It was hard to keep the facts straight in her head.

Her own mom was wreathed in smiles. *Gulp.* Her dad was nowhere to be seen, thank goodness. Hopefully he didn't know anything about this whole affair. James still seemed to think that her stepdad was her real father. Since her mom also acted as if he was, and had changed Fiona's surname to his, the illusion was easy to maintain.

Afterward she offered to accompany her mom and stepdad back to the hotel, but James stepped in. "I'm afraid that won't be possible." Mischief glittered in his eyes. "I've made alternative arrangements."

Her mom gave her a conspiratorial smile. "Well, we can hardly argue with your future husband."

Fiona opened her mouth, but no words came out.

Guests were filing out through the grand doors. Her mom and stepdad walked off, smiling. James's mom was long gone. All the business bigwigs Fiona had been paraded in front of were heading off toward their chauffeured cars. Soon she and James would be left alone. "What did you have in mind?" Her voice sounded annoyingly high and nervous.

"That's for me to know and you to find out while it's happening."

"What if I don't like surprises?"

"I already know you better than that." His mouth looked unbearably kissable. "That's why you're coming with me." He threaded his arm through hers and marched her out through the glittering foyer.

His driver whisked them back to his penthouse in record time.

"Should I be seen coming up to your place before the wedding?" She glanced around at the empty street as they drove up to the apartment complex.

"Definitely not. That's why I told Al to park inside. We'll take the internal elevator up." His seductive smile tugged at his lips.

"You're a bad influence."

"Sorry." He didn't sound at all contrite.

Her skin tingled with the prospect of having James's hands on it. And damn, but she was curious to get a closer look at where and how he lived. She'd seen the Scottish place he inherited, but this was the castle he'd chosen for himself and she'd only had a small glimpse of it her first time here.

On her first visit she'd come through the lobby, but this time they took an elevator from the enclosed car park that opened directly into his apartment. The soaring space looked out over the harbor, where lights twinkled on the water. The floor was a smooth, honed marble and the furnishings sleek and modern but comfortable-looking. A grand piano stood near the window. "Do you play?" She walked toward it. Wow, it was a Steinway, probably over a hundred years old, and worth... She couldn't even imagine. Her fingers itched to touch the ivory keys.

"A little."

"Will you play something for me?"

"All right." He shrugged off his suit jacket and flung it over a chair, then sat on the elegant piano stool. His fingers skated over the keys, and then he plunged into a dramatic piece she recognized vaguely. Debussy, maybe? His powerful hands seemed to span the keyboard effortlessly, and music from the magnificent instrument filled the air.

Great. One more reason James Drummond was too good to be true. He ended with a flourish. "Would you like to try?"

"Uh, sure." She sat down and acted as if she was about to play chopsticks. Then she tested the first few keys of her favorite sonata. She glanced at James. He was grinning. "Go on. You're far too competitive not to top my performance." His voice was gruff with pleasure.

She laughed. "You do know me well, but unfortunately you'll be hard to outdo." She let her fingers flow over the keys, and closed her eyes as the music drifted around her. The piece seemed to play itself, sound swelling through her whole body and filling the room. When she'd finished she opened her eyes as if waking from a dream.

"Not bad." His eyes sparkled. He extended a hand and she took it as she stood, feeling even sadder that she wasn't marrying James and his incredible piano. "As I suspected, you could probably have a career as a concert pianist. Now, preliminaries aside, let's head for the bedroom."

She laughed. "You're a hard man to argue with, James Drummond."

His bedroom was very large, with a low platform bed covered with a plush white duvet. A contrast of soft and hard, much like its handsome owner.

They undressed each other slowly, savoring every moment as anticipation built in the air. "It feels like a year since I've touched you properly." James's voice was husky.

"At least a year." Her skin hummed under his fingers. How many more encounters would they have before James knew the truth about her and hated her? Her heart ached with regret for things that hadn't even happened yet.

But that didn't dim her desire to press her body against his and drink in his warm, masculine scent. His arms circled around her waist and made her feel strangely protected.

Which was ridiculous. Some primeval instincts kicked in whenever James was around and short-circuited all common sense. His warm breath brushed her cheek and sent a thrill of arousal through her. She loved how tall he was, the broadness of his chest, the strong jut of his jaw. There was something so noble about him—entirely aside from his noble ancestry—that made her feel very feminine.

He kissed her, and that familiar rush of excitement rose inside her. How would she manage when this was all over? Would anyone ever kiss her like this again?

She felt her breathing quicken as a growing sense of panic mixed with her desire.

"I want you." It seemed safe to say that. The words sounded noncommittal, purely sexual, a confession of desire. But behind them hid a deeper well of longing. She did want James. She wanted to be with him, to talk to him, to touch him, to make love. If things had been different, who knows? They might have had a future together.

At least they had this moment, happening right now in all its complex and breathless glory. She unbuttoned his shirt and pulled it off, then licked the contours of his chest. He unzipped her dress and tugged it gently over her head, then painted invisible decorations on her breasts and belly with his tongue.

Her whole body felt alive with sensation. James was a very deliberate lover, both careful and creative, much the way he must be in business. He sought out her magic buttons with determination and pressed them in ways that made her cry out and sigh and beg him to stop— and not to stop.

She loved the salty taste of his skin, the slight roughness of his hair and the hard, masculine ridges of his muscles. She searched for his secret erogenous zones and was rewarded with deep groans and sharp gasps when she discovered a new one. Her competitive instincts compelled her to drive him even more wild and crazy than he'd driven her, and the results were impressive and addictive. They were both ready to explode—or implode—by the time he entered her, but they managed to prolong the delicious agony for just the right amount of time before finally letting go.

She had *never* had sex like this.

Fiona had never felt so well matched with a partner.

James's driven and meticulous nature suited her own so perfectly. Maybe they were meant to be together, and all these other things—the factory, her dad, the missing cup—were mere distractions on the road to them living happily ever after. When they lay together in each other's arms, it seemed impossible that something so trivial as a business deal could separate them.

Maybe she really did need to find that damn cup fragment to break the curse hanging over the Drummonds and pave the way for James's future to blend happily with her own. She wanted him to be happy. She wanted herself to be happy. Perhaps she could just come clean with him about the factory and make a deal to buy it from him so her dad could be happy, too.

But then he'd figure out all her angles. He'd know she had an agenda and react with disgust and she'd lose it all. At least if she persisted with her original plan she'd end up being closer to her dad, which was of course her primary goal.

"Oh, James." It was so strange to rest her head on his chest while all these crazy, treacherous thoughts scrambled through her brain. And she didn't know what was running around in *his* brain. She knew he wasn't marrying her for love, but for some reasons of his own. There was nothing natural and organic about their courtship. It had all the hallmarks of a high-stakes merger.

He stroked her hair, and her thoughts drifted away again. If only she could make this moment last for a month, or a year. She just wanted to rest awhile and inhale the scent of his skin.

But she wasn't cut out for resting. "That old factory building…" The words crept out of her mouth almost of their own accord.

"The one we walked past?"

"Yes." She hoped he wouldn't notice her heart beating faster. Or that he'd blame it on the amazing sex.

"How much would you sell that for?"

He laughed, which shook his chest under her cheek. "I wouldn't."

"How about a ridiculous price?"

"The ridiculous price would still be less than what it's worth once I develop it. I've had my team watching that property and planning the acquisition for nearly two years. I have a lot of time and energy invested in it."

"Oh." Much as she'd suspected all along. Should she push harder and possibly reveal her hand? At some point, she had to. "What if I wanted it as my prize if I win the race?"

She held her breath. She couldn't see his face from this angle, but she could imagine his eyes narrowing into his characteristic thoughtful expression.

"In that case, I could hardly say no." She heard amusement in his tone. Probably because he expected to win. Men like James always expected to win, regardless of the odds. It was probably a key reason why they usually did win. But she had the advantage of being light, and fiendishly determined.

In not saying no, he'd said *yes*.

Maybe she could win the race, give the factory to her dad, marry James, then live happily ever after and laugh long and loud about the whole thing. If handled delicately it was possible. He'd already agreed to turn it over if she won. Now all she had to do was win fair and square.

I want to marry him. The realization made her toes curl. She liked this man so much. Loved him? That could be the strange feeling unfurling in her chest and befuddling her usually sharp brain. She could easily see them enjoying each other's company for many years to come. Maybe his own decisiveness in choosing her as his bride came from a similar intense conviction that she was the one for him.

She slid up his chest and kissed his mouth, which smiled beneath her lips.

"You really want that factory?"

She shrugged, pretending to be casual. "I think it would be perfect for·me."

"You're on."

Her heart soared. Suddenly, it seemed as if she could have it all. The factory, her father's appreciation and affection, and James—happily ever after. She always had been lucky. After all, anyone who made as much money as she had at such a young age was good at pulling rabbits out of hats.

She kissed James again, enjoying the shiver of lust that licked through her when she tasted him. *She could do this.*

As long as she didn't look down. Raw nerve, skilled riding and tight lips. She'd have to pull it all together and make that race the triumph of a lifetime. No pressure, of course. Just her life and several others hanging in the balance. In a few more days, her future would be determined, for better or worse.

Nine

An early-morning drizzle had left the Scottish landscape lush and fragrant. A hazy sun now dried the dew on the castle walls.

"The horses have had plenty of time to digest their breakfast." James glanced at her. "Are you getting cold feet?" He was teasing but also concerned. The race as they'd planned it would be long, hard and not a little dangerous. If she wanted to back out he was absolutely fine with it.

He could hardly believe he'd promised to give her that piece of land as a prize. Part of him knew she wouldn't win. The other part of him wanted her to win so he could see what she'd do with it.

"Not at all." She tilted her chin. "Just want to make sure they're ready."

"I think that will be the least of their problems." They'd bandaged their legs for protection from brush and support for their tendons. The horses were fit and sleek and had been exercised every day that week by the grooms. "Are you sure you want to ride Taffy? Solomon's quite a bit faster. He was bred for racing, whereas Taffy was bred for hunting."

"That's why Taffy will give me an edge over the rough country." She looked utterly confident, sure she'd win. And maybe she would. His competitive nature ensured that he'd give her the best run he could. On his faster horse, and with his knowledge of the countryside, he was almost sure to beat her, but he admired her ambition to try.

"You have the satellite phone on you?" He wanted to make sure she could reach help if needed. He intended to stay within earshot of her, but wanted to be prepared for anything.

"In my inside pocket." She patted her vest. "Right next to the rabbit's foot and the four-leaf clover."

He laughed. "You don't seem the superstitious type."

"You haven't known me that long. I'm superstitious enough to know that you can't beat me with the curse of your ancestors hanging over you. Maybe it's part of my strategy to make sure you couldn't find that cup piece."

She took the reins from the groom and mounted Taffy. He watched with pleasure as her lithe, athletic body settled lightly in the saddle.

"You know I don't believe in any of that. My life has been working out just fine with the damned thing missing all these years. Besides, both my cousins seem to have suddenly found love and happiness without any help from the cup." He heaved himself back into the saddle.

"Are these the two cousins who located their missing pieces of the cup?"

"Yes, but the curse isn't lifted until all three parts of the cup are reunited."

"Hmm. Then I guess they're doomed to divorce and loneliness unless we find the piece that's here in Scotland."

James frowned as an odd feeling twisted his gut. Maybe it was apprehension about the race. Solomon shifted his weight and felt restless, and he patted the horse's neck to soothe him. Would his cousins—both close in age to him—avoid the disappointment and disasters of their forebears? He certainly had no intention of going down that road. That's why he'd chosen a wife with his head, not his heart.

Though his heart certainly did beat fast as he watched her take the lead down the drive in front of him. "Do you remember the route?"

"The entire estate boundary, counterclockwise."

"It'll take about five hours."

"I know. I plan to pace myself." She looked downright cocky. He still didn't know how she'd learned to ride so well. She said she'd done some endurance rides in the hills of California, but he didn't imagine they'd give her too much preparation for the rugged Scottish landscape. Or the Scottish weather. "Did you pack a raincoat?"

"Would you stop fussing!" She turned around and rested one hand on her horse's rump, while still moving forward at a brisk walk. "I'll be fine. And I'm going to win." Her bright smile sent a jolt of excitement through him.

"No way."

"Just watch me." She shot him a cheeky grin.

"I wish I could, but I don't want to look back over my shoulder while I'm galloping." He walked his horse faster until they were abreast. "Giles is going to call the start." Giles, the groom, walked a few paces behind them. "Firing a pistol might get the horses too excited."

"I want my horse excited." She stroked Taffy's big neck. "But don't worry. I'll get her there without any help from firearms." James was glad she'd agreed to ride Taffy. The big mare would take care of her. She certainly wasn't the fastest horse in the stable, but with her extensive hunting experience and sturdy build, she was the least likely to run into unexpected lameness or to spook and throw her rider, and those things generally meant more when it came to reaching the finish line in a long race.

"Are you going to let me win?" She'd turned to face him again, and pinned him with a fierce look.

"Never. The honor of the Drummonds rests on my victory." He slammed a fist to his chest.

Okay, so maybe at that exact moment he had been wondering if he should let her stay out in front, just so he could watch her and make sure she didn't do anything rash and dangerous. What was he thinking? Did he actually want to give up that nice piece of property so close to Orchard Road? He laughed. He must be going soft. Or else he was falling hard for Fiona. "I promise that if you win you'll do it fair and square."

"Good, because I do plan to win and I don't want you telling yourself that it was all your idea."

"Stone wall is your mark." Giles's gruff voice pierced the air. A low stone wall divided the manicured lawn nearest the house from the first stretch of rough pasture. They pulled their horses up in the gateway. Both mounts were clearly excited and ready to blow off some steam, no doubt taking some unconscious cues from their riders.

"Are you ready?" Both answered Giles's question with an unwavering "yes."

"On your marks, get set… Go!" The horses leaped into action, thundering across the field at a canter. The sky was bright, pale blue with a few fluffy white clouds, and the sun half blinded him as they headed toward the eastern boundary of the estate.

To his chagrin he noticed Fiona had already risen out of the saddle into a light two-point, and seemed to float effortlessly over her horse. His nearly two hundred pounds of solid muscle, however, moved with his horse's back as they cleared the first rise. She'd get tired standing up like that, wouldn't she? For the first time he wondered if she really had a chance of beating him.

The prospect only fired his more aggressive urges, and he cued Solomon into a gallop and passed her.

"Don't wear your horse out too quickly!" she called, a bright tone in her voice.

"Don't you worry about us," he shouted back over his shoulder. "Solomon and I have the whole race planned out." He led the way to the broad ditch that marked the first boundary, then crossed it and rode along the wide top of the berm his ancestors must have dug over a thousand—maybe even two thousand—years ago. They'd claimed their territory with sweat and soil, and the markers they'd made persisted through countless political regimes and monarchies. He intended to see that they'd survive intact another thousand years, even if he'd rather be sailing his yacht in Singapore.

A sense of duty. That's what propelled a family like the Drummonds to survive and thrive from one generation to the next. Curses didn't have much impact on sheer determination, even if one were to believe in them.

The sound of Taffy's sturdy hoofbeats reassured him as they set out on the first stretch, running right along the eastern border, between the pastures of the estate and the uncultivated wilderness beyond. There was room for two horses to pass, but it would take some nerve, like passing from the inside lane on a racetrack.

He wasn't surprised when Fiona tried it a few minutes in. "Outside," she called, then he heard a quickening of footfalls and Taffy eased past him into the lead. Adrenaline fired through him, urging him to take back the lead, but he forced himself to hold back.

She was safer out in front where he could keep an eye on her. And damn, that was some view to behold. Her tight, shapely backside poised gracefully above Taffy's powerful hindquarters.

He could take the lead back at any time, he reassured himself. He just didn't want to.

Yet.

The exhilaration of galloping—and making sure it was still a controlled and sustainable gallop—sent thrills surging to Fiona's toes and fingers. Passing James had given her a rush of excitement, and she could almost imagine being a jockey in the Grand National, heading for the finish line in front of a crowd of cheering fans.

Except that here there were no spectators beyond a lone eagle and the occasional rabbit darting in the wild brush to her right.

"Don't take the hill too fast." James's voice came through the wind.

The wide swale dipped and followed the contour of the landscape downward. A valley spread out below them, with a winding river at the bottom. "This view is distracting," she shouted. She slowed Taffy to a trot as she negotiated the hill. It wasn't really that steep, but why take a chance? Taffy was James's horse, after all, and even if she weren't his, Fiona didn't want her to slip and get hurt.

The berm bridged the river at the bottom, a roiling, foaming current, and then swooped upward again. James almost passed her at the foot of it, but she laughed and spurred Taffy back into a gallop, whipping past him and tackling the smooth, sheep-mowed turf with ease. "It's lucky for me your horses are kept so fit."

"I like them to be ready for anything," he yelled back.

"Conquering neighboring estates?"

"You never know."

She grinned. It was easy to imagine James leading an army into battle, pennants fluttering in the wind and horses snorting. His ancestors had probably done just that to gain this huge tract of land and defend it over the centuries. No wonder James could never abandon the place entirely for a Singapore penthouse. If it were hers she probably wouldn't ever want to leave.

If it were hers.

And it could be, if she were James's wife. Her dad would eventually get used to the idea that she'd married James. Sooner or later the two most important men in her life would become friends and would laugh about their rivalry for the factory and the land under it. As the wind whipped her face and the bright sky dazzled her eyes, it seemed inevitable that everything should work out just the way she envisioned.

"Go on, Taffy," she urged as they climbed another small rise and took a turn to the left. She had to win. If she didn't win, her entire carefully wrought plan would fall apart.

When they reached a particularly rocky stretch of landscape, the berm morphed into a stone wall, and suddenly they were cantering neck and neck alongside it over a field of tufted grass.

"Your horse looks tired," she called.

"Solomon's not even on his second wind yet." James grinned and urged his horse ahead. As Solomon's swirling black tail pulled level with Taffy's neck, Fiona's stomach tightened. For a brief second, she could feel it all slipping away—the factory, her dad, her future with James, so she dug her heels into Taffy's sides and pushed the big horse forward, stretching her out until she peeled past them. Now was the time to take advantage of her lighter weight and put some real distance between them. She could see the castle to her left, and could tell they were now coming down the western boundary. There was almost no way to get lost from here. If she could pull ahead of him and gain a real edge, she'd be that much closer to winning.

She moved past him and sped forward as fast as she could. The sound of Solomon's footfalls grew distant, and when she glanced back over her shoulder she could see them fifty yards away, then a hundred. She couldn't keep this pace up for long without exhausting her horse, so she waited until she was just far enough ahead then steadied her pace. He'd obviously done the same as he wasn't catching up with her.

She grinned, taking in the spectacular view of the rugged landscape and the mossy towers of the castle. With a little planning and determination, she could accomplish almost anything in life.

As Fiona disappeared from sight around the bend on the homestretch, James came to a very unsettling realization. He wanted her to win. The desire to have someone else come out ahead in a contest went against all his training and experience. His boarding school had drilled him in the ruthless crushing of opponents of all kinds. For years he'd schooled himself to focus intently on his goal. Collateral damage could be cleaned up later. He rarely failed to clinch a deal, even if it took several years to get all the parties and the funding lined up and on the same page.

And now he was planning to let Fiona beat him on his home turf and to give her the prime piece of real estate he'd had his eye on for years.

Clearly she had a profound effect on him.

"You're driving me crazy." He said the words into the wind, knowing there was no way she could hear them. She was too far ahead. His heart swelled at the sight of her cantering steadily along on Taffy as if she could do it all day. Which she obviously could.

They'd been riding since midmorning and it was now late afternoon. She clearly intended to win. He loved that!

He never thought he'd meet a woman as focused and determined as himself. Her success in business had intrigued him in the first place, her beauty and intelligence had hooked him, and she'd turned out to be even more fabulous than he'd imagined. The cursory background research he'd done showed an uneventful childhood in California, peppered with academic successes that led to a spectacular four years at a top university, just as he'd anticipated. Then she'd started her first business and turned it into an international sensation. Fiona Lam was an amazing woman.

Solomon was blowing beneath him, probably relaxing in the knowledge that his stall and a long drink of

water weren't too far away now. "Come on, boy, not
long now. Shall we put on a burst of speed so it looks
like we're trying?"

Solomon obliged, and soon James glimpsed Taffy's
pale rump rising and falling through the thin copse of
trees that led to the drive. "I'm going to beat you!" He
couldn't resist the last-minute challenge.

Fiona whipped her head around, then crouched
lower over Taffy, urging her to go faster. He laughed
and enjoyed the view as Solomon lumbered across the
last stretch of open pasture toward the stable yard.
Fiona galloped up the last rise as if her life depended
on it, then thrust up an arm in triumph as she reached
the top.

He slowed Solomon to a walk. Fiona had jumped off
and was giving Taffy a hug. Two grooms rushed forward, ready to cool out the tired horses.

"I told you I'd win." Her cheeks glowed pink as she
stood, hands on hips. Her pale jodhpurs and tall boots
were splashed with mud.

"And you were right. I'm duly impressed. Solomon
and I will have to eat humble pie for dinner."

"I'm a lot lighter than you." He felt her eyes on his
more massive frame as he eased himself down from
Solomon and hit the ground with a thud.

"There's no arguing with that." He wanted to kiss her
right here. Why not? He took her in his arms, and the
taste of her mouth was like champagne after the long,
arduous ride. She held him tight, her breath coming
in unsteady gasps. When they finally pulled apart, he
studied her face. "This race really meant a lot to you."

"I don't like to lose."

"Well, you didn't. You have my undying admiration, and now a piece of land in Singapore."

Her eyes sparkled. "I'm thrilled. By both. Kiss me again!"

The extreme athletic feat of winning the race sucked the wind out of Fiona. She could barely make it through dinner without closing her eyes. A long bubble bath and an early night in James's arms should have been the perfect ending to a spectacular day.

But a nasty sense of foreboding crept over her. James needed to go back to Singapore for a meeting, and while she ached to go with him, she knew it was a bad idea.

"What's the matter?" James tried to massage her shoulders, but they kept tying themselves back into knots.

"Oh, nothing. I'm just tired."

"Are you sure you want to stay here while I'm in Singapore?"

"Definitely. I'm determined to find the missing cup piece. I think it will bring us good luck." She couldn't face the thought of going back there and being thrust into the whole engagement whirlwind again. Not until it felt real. "As long as there's a car I can use to get around I'll be fine."

"Angus will keep one fueled and ready for you. When you grow bored with rifling through old junk you can join me in Singapore and we can finalize the wedding details together."

"Do you really have to leave today? Stay here awhile longer. Change your meeting to next week." Suddenly she was terrified of losing him.

"I wish I could but it's a deal I've been working on

literally for years. It's with Goh Kwon Beng, the man I introduced you to the other day."

"Oh." She had a weird feeling that this meeting had something to do with their impending marriage, though she couldn't imagine how. And why did that sound so much like impending doom? The mention was a sharp reminder that he was marrying her in a rush for reasons of his own. He didn't love her. There were no promises of undying affection between them. Really they were just starting to date and get to know each other under intense pressure—from both sides. "I'll miss you." It was the truth.

"I'll miss you, too." He kissed her again, so softly it was almost like a breath.

Hopefully by the time he came back she'd have pacified her father by telling him the land was his. Maybe then this could turn into a real relationship without all the underhanded drama. Still, she needed to tie up the scheme first. "Will you send me the deed for the land?"

"I have it right here, in my briefcase. I can't believe I forgot about it." He eased off the bed, naked, and walked to the far side of the room. He reached into a dark leather satchel and pulled out a plain manila envelope. "Here it is. It's yours."

"I can't believe you have it here. You're too funny."

"I'm always deadly serious."

"I like that about you." He was truly a man of his word, someone you could count on, even under these rather bizarre circumstances. Her hand trembled slightly when she took the envelope. How would James react if he knew that their entire relationship, even their first meeting, had been engineered to obtain this one document?

For now, at least, it would be her secret.

"It's sweet of you to let me stay here." He obviously trusted her. A trust that was not entirely justified.

"I'm counting on you to find the cup fragment so we can enjoy a glorious future together, unlike most of the Drummonds. Katherine's phoned or emailed me nearly every day. If nothing else it will make her happy."

She bit her lip.

"What's the matter?"

"What if I don't find it?"

"That's not the Fiona I know and…" He stopped short before uttering the word *love,* but it hung in the air anyway and reverberated like a freshly banged gong.

Love. Would it grow between them naturally and organically once the pressure was off? Or were they doomed to the fate of most Drummond men and their unfortunate spouses? Her breathing felt shallow.

"You'll find it. I have complete confidence in you." James climbed back onto the bed with her. His nearness was reassuring. She dreaded tomorrow, when he'd leave and she'd be all alone. Too much time to think and worry.

"I'll do my best." Perhaps that cup really was the key to James—and her—finding happiness.

"I'm counting on you."

Don't count on me, she wanted to say. *I'm not the person you think I am at all. I'm a devious, cunning stranger who cajoled my way into your innermost sanctum for my own purposes.* But she didn't say any of that. Instead, she touched his rough cheek with her fingers and kissed him on the mouth, as emotions tangled in her heart.

"Dad, remember not to tell anyone how you got it." She was walking along the battlements on the roof of the oldest part of the castle while talking on the phone. At least there she knew no one could listen in. The dramatic landscape stretched in all directions, making her feel very small. A cold snap had painted the hills with a russet tinge. Why wouldn't time stand still?

"Why not? It's a funny story. Besides, you're all done with that devil now. You can tell him where to shove it."

She hesitated. How did she tell her dad that she'd grown to like James?

To love him.

Okay. Maybe you couldn't really love someone on this short acquaintance, but she liked him more than any man she'd ever met, and if passion was a measure of any kind…

"James and I… I don't want him to know the whole story." Suddenly her delicate house of cards was in danger of falling apart. Maybe if she could buy a little time? "The taxes are paid through the end of next year. If you sit on it quietly until then there'll be time for me to smooth things over."

"But I need to reopen my factory." Her father sounded almost petulant.

"It didn't make any money." Now she was whining, too. "Just wait awhile and we'll work on a new project together. I'd like to start a retail business in Singapore, and I know you're the perfect person to help me with it. It's an ideal spot, so near Orchard Road and I…"

"I had orders. I can be back in business by the end of the month. All the machinery is still there."

Her heart sank. Her dad was so stubborn. Then again, she'd told him she'd get him his factory back, not that she'd tell him what to do with it. She'd already sent the deed to him via DHL. Smoothing things over with James was her problem alone. "Dad, James put a lot of trust in me, and I need a few weeks to straighten things out." With time she could think of some way to present it that sounded less mercenary. Or at least by then the engagement and marriage train would have hurtled so far forward that it would be less likely to wreck and fall off the tracks. "Promise me you won't tell anyone, not for a little while."

"Oh, Fiona, you're such a worrier. Just like your mother."

Thoughts of Fiona crowded James's mind in her absence. He found himself dreaming about their future and making plans he'd never even discussed with her. Names for their children, even the schools those imaginary children might attend.

He seemed to be living and breathing every minute in a state of suspended animation until he could hold her in his arms again.

Which was why the headline of Wednesday's paper came as such a brutal shock.

James sat down hard in his chair. His office seemed to shrink around him, as his whole world transformed into an alien landscape quite different from the one he thought he was living in.

Drummond Engagement a Ruse. The headline mocked him. The article itself devastated him.

Fiona had given the land to her father. Given it *back* to her father. A father he never even knew existed, since his rudimentary peek into Fiona's past had told him only what he wanted to hear. A father who now claimed—from every rooftop—that their entire romance was a scheme to reclaim his "stolen" property.

James's first instinct was to argue with the media. To claim that it couldn't be true. Fiona would never do that! But he knew immediately, in his own rather stony heart, that it was not only possible, but utterly true.

Fiona never intended to marry him at all. Which explained why she didn't want to choose her wedding dress, or even tell her parents about their intended marriage. Because there wasn't going to be a wedding.

He'd chosen her as his wife and rushed their courtship forward to secure his long-awaited business deal with Goh Kwon Beng, and it had never occurred to him that she had her own reasons for agreeing to such a precipitous engagement. Easily distracted by her business reputation and the stellar educational record she'd blazed in California, he'd done his research with blinders on. He'd been looking for good things and found them, so confident and intent on achieving his own goals that he'd walked right into a trap.

Fiona's ruthless determination and fearless pursuit of her goals had intrigued and attracted him. Now he was surprised that they'd been used against him? He should curse himself for being a fool.

She didn't answer his calls that morning. Hardly surprising. He hadn't been able to get hold of her the night before, either. Someone in Singapore must have told her the story would run. Maybe she even planted it herself.

Now he was forced to ask his household staff about her whereabouts. He could hardly believe he'd left a virtual stranger unattended in his ancestral home. Except that she was supposed to be his fiancée and the castle was intended to be her home, too.

"Angus, uh, is everything okay with Fiona?" How did you delicately ask if your intended bride was still there?

"I drove her to the airport this morning. She should be back with you soon."

"Oh, yes, I'm sure she'll be here any minute," he lied. Where was she going? Likely not back to Singapore, at least not yet. She didn't seem the type to court this kind of publicity. Unless she really did want to crow over him and celebrate her victory. "Thanks, Angus."

He didn't believe there was malice behind it. Then again, maybe that was more evidence of his stupidity in this whole situation. He'd had such a great time with her. He didn't remember ever enjoying a woman's company like this before. And the sex they'd had was in its own league. She'd enjoyed it, too. Had her pleasure been simply in a mercenary victory over an adversary?

Damn, but he wanted to talk to her and hear her side of the story. But even in this high-tech world, he didn't know a way to compel a free citizen to answer her phone when she didn't want to speak to you.

Ten

James had left several messages on her phone since she'd fled the estate earlier this morning. She couldn't even bear to listen to them anymore so she let the battery run out and dropped the phone in a garbage can at the airport. If she had any human decency at all she'd call him and explain her side of the story. She'd tell him she really did have feelings for him. She'd beg for forgiveness and they'd live happily ever after.

But this was James Drummond she'd made a fool of. The tone of his messages was confused at first, then angry, then a cold, deadly fury. She'd known she was taking on a powerful adversary when she walked into this whole situation. That's why she'd planned to disappear to California once she got her dad's factory back.

She'd since dared to dream that she and James could have a real future together. But when a reporter from a Singapore daily had called her looking for salacious tidbits about their romance, she'd learned that the story would break, and her courage failed her.

The ending of this story had been planned since their first meeting, but she hadn't intended for it to hurt like being cut open with a knife.

The journey back to California went way too fast. Racked by guilt and sorrow, she couldn't look forward to anything. Her friend Crystal told her she could stay as long as she liked, so at least she had a place to hide, but even seeing her old friends couldn't distract Fiona from the misery of losing James just when she'd realized she wanted to keep him forever.

The day after she arrived, Crystal tried to console her over margaritas at their favorite tapas bar. "You said from the beginning that it was a business thing. You accomplished your goal. You should be celebrating, not looking like you're about to weep more salt into the olives."

"I am not going to weep." The sharp margarita stung her tongue. Besides, she'd done enough weeping already; she was just too ashamed to admit it. "He turned out to be so much…cooler than I was expecting."

"You had fun with him." Crystal tipped her head to the side, and her long braids almost brushed the table.

"Way too much fun." The restaurant stereo was playing The Eagles's "Hotel California," which didn't help her gloomy mood. "How many men have I ever met who can even ride a horse let alone race with me all day on one?" She shook her head. "I was even crazy enough to think he might be the one. And you can imagine how insane I'd have to be to think that while I'm pursuing a scheme to separate him from his property."

Crystal sighed. "That is pretty crazy. The sex must have been sensational."

She nodded. "Totally. I can't imagine I'll ever have sex like that again. There was a real connection between us."

"Maybe there still is?" Crystal picked up a shrimp and dipped it in spicy sauce. "I think you should reach out to him and tell him how you feel."

"No way." She frowned. "You didn't hear the messages he left me. He was furious. And why wouldn't he be? I read some of the articles online. My dad made sure James came out looking like a fool. He didn't just lose out on a business deal. He had the supposed woman of his dreams thumb her nose at him in the press. That's probably the ultimate in humiliation for a guy."

"You didn't do that."

"My dad made it seem like I did, and for someone in the public eye it amounts to the same thing." Now anger warred with all the other conflicting emotions. She'd waited so long and worked so hard to win her dad's affections. Now he'd betrayed her.

"Damn. I sure hope your dad is grateful for what you did."

She swallowed. "I've tried calling him several times this week and I haven't heard back. I phoned to ask if the deed arrived safely, and he didn't even respond. I had to check DHL tracking to make sure it wasn't lost somewhere." Maybe he didn't want to talk to her now that he'd done exactly what she begged him not to.

"You're kidding!" Crystal's horrified stare made her look away. "Has he even said thank you?"

"I'm sure he's grateful. It's just that…" That what? She'd been so sure that winning back his factory would make her a heroine in her dad's eyes. That it could somehow compensate for all the missed years together and draw them close in the father-daughter relationship she'd dreamed of. Now her long-cherished dream—put into very real action—seemed like a foolish fantasy. Once again her dad was immersed in his own busy universe and had no time for her, exactly as her mom and Crystal had warned her.

"He used you."

"Nonsense. The entire thing was my idea." She sipped her margarita and relished the cool sting on her tongue. "I have no one to blame but myself. I wanted to help my dad. I wanted to make him like me. I never for one moment thought about James's feelings when I embarked on this whole thing."

"Well, you had no idea he was going to ask you to marry him. That part was all his fault."

"I know, and I'm sure it was a business thing for him to marry me. He has some important deal coming up with a guy named Beng who doesn't appreciate fast-living bachelors. He was totally using me for his own reasons. But that doesn't make me feel any better. I know he did intend to marry me."

"What did you do with the ring?" Crystal raised a pierced brow.

"The engagement ring." She squeezed her eyes shut for a moment. "Jeez. I never did tell him where I left it." She cringed at the sudden realization that he might think she'd taken it. "I put it in the top drawer of a chest in the bedroom I stayed in at the castle. I knew I had to leave it but I didn't want the staff to find it. I'll have to tell him somehow." Her heart felt like lead.

"Write to him."

"An email?" She'd blocked his address after a barrage of angry *call me*'s came through.

"No, not an email. An old-fashioned epistle."

"A pen-and-paper letter?" Fiona paused. The idea

appealed to her. It didn't have the frightening possibility of an instant and hostile response the way email and the phone did. There would be time for her to choose her words carefully, and time for him to think about his response. If he even wanted to dignify her letter with a response. "You might be onto something."

She sat up late into the night, writing and rewriting, crumpling the pages and throwing them away. It was a long time since she'd written a letter on paper, and she worried that he wouldn't be able to read her chicken scratch.

She knew he wouldn't forgive her. The Singapore media was still making fun of him, and she'd just read online about Beng's SK Industries forming an alliance with another local entrepreneur—an older family man with three teenage daughters—for the purpose of aggressive real-estate acquisition. In addition to making him a laughingstock in the gossip columns, she'd ruined James's plans to partner with Singapore's Mr. Big.

She owed him an explanation. There was no way she could handle talking to him on the phone. She was too ashamed of her own duplicity for that. Email seemed too impersonal, and at the same time too immediate and close to a phone call. The prospect of her letter traveling slowly by air like a leisurely bird, and alighting at its destination to face its fate—that seemed doable.

Dear James,

Even that part was hard. Did she have the nerve to call him "dear" after the way she'd used him?

I'm not asking for forgiveness, or even acknowledgment of this letter. I freely admit that I'm too chicken to talk to you directly, which is why I've avoided your calls. I didn't mean for it to work out this way.

Was that last line really true? When she'd started out she'd fully intended an ending like this.

When my father first told me he'd lost his business, I discovered what had happened and wanted to help. I didn't talk to you about my father, for obvious reasons, but we've been estranged for most of my life and I desperately wanted—and still want—to form a close relationship with him.

Would James understand? He'd never had a close relationship with his own father.

When an acquaintance pointed you out to me at that party, I formed a sudden resolution to get to know you and convince you to sell me the property. My dad had warned me you'd never sell, and as I got to know you, I discovered that he was right. Everything you do is done for a reason, and you rarely if ever backtrack on a course you've started. When you offered me the opportunity to come to Scotland, I couldn't believe my luck.

No one could accuse her of being sensible. And maybe the worst part was how the Scottish countryside had taken hold of her. The once-loved hills of California now seemed dry and bare, the bright sun too harsh. She missed that cloud-scudded sky and the bright patchwork of green and gray and rich brown, with its splashes of bright heather. It would be hard to come up with pretexts to visit Scotland on a regular basis. Now, in addition to missing James, she'd have to nurse an inconvenient longing for a place she didn't belong to, and never would.

Things quickly spiraled out of control. When you asked me to marry you, I knew I couldn't achieve my goals unless I said yes. I know you must have had your own reasons for wanting to marry someone you'd barely met and in such a hurry. I suspect your reasons were almost as mercenary as mine, but the difference remains: you planned to marry me, and I didn't intend to marry you. Therefore you were honest in your actions, and I wasn't. Am I ashamed of how I played along? Absolutely. I could plead that I changed my mind and really did want to marry you by the time of the race, but the fact remains that obtaining my father's former property back remained my main goal, and I was obviously willing to risk everything in pursuit of it.

I wish things could have worked out differently. I was hoping that my father could wait quietly for a while until we were married and happy together, and then I could tell you everything and hope that you'd understand, but he couldn't resist the urge to crow over his "enemy." I'm well aware that the embarrassment you suffered in the press is entirely my fault and I am truly sorry for that.

Again, I don't ask for your forgiveness, I just wanted to respond to your calls in the cowardly way that is all I can apparently handle.

I love you.

She didn't write that. That would add insult to injury and seem phony beyond belief, even if it was true.

I wish I had found that cup piece because I do want you to have a happy future, and I know that I must seem like a manifestation of the Drummond curse. If there was a way to make things better, I'd offer to try, but my imagination fails me.

Although that race led to a disastrous fallout between us, I'm afraid I shall always cherish it as one of the best days of my life.

No mention of the incredible sex. She wouldn't be forgetting that anytime soon, either. Her whole body ached as she thought about spending the rest of her life without ever feeling James's arms around her again.

Would she do it all again? No way. But at least now she knew how intense and wonderful things could be with the right kind of man.

James wasn't the right man. If he was, things wouldn't have crashed and burned the way they did. Each had their own agenda that trumped the personal side of their relationship. His business deal was no doubt more important than any affection they had for each other. She knew that. It made her feel a tiny bit better.

But not much.

I hope you find the perfect woman to spend the rest of your life with. Go slower next time and get to know her before you ask her to marry you.

Her advice seemed a little obnoxious, but she didn't want him to make the same mistake twice. Women weren't like a business where you could just rush in and start giving orders and expect everything to go well. And he needed someone strong and independent—like her.

She sighed. They really were a good match. But not good enough.

I wish you all the best,
Fiona

She sealed the envelope and wrote his Singapore address on it. Then remembered she hadn't mentioned the ring, so she had to rip it open.

P.S. I left the engagement ring in the top drawer of the carved dresser in my bedroom.

My bedroom? What was she thinking? But she didn't want to rewrite the whole letter now. It had taken about thirty-two drafts to get this far.

It is a lovely ring and hope they will take it back.

Again she cringed. He'd have to take it back himself or ask one of the staff to do it—either way would be very embarrassing for him. Yet she hated the idea of that lovely ring sitting around the castle gathering dust. Or worse yet, ending up on someone else's finger. She'd much rather it went back to the shop and was disassembled to its component parts and maybe turned into a nice brooch.

She blew out hard, wrote out a new envelope and sealed it up. Her dad had answered her latest call with a gruff announcement that he was busy and would call her soon. That was ten days ago. People often ditched the friend who helped them out of a tough spot, because that person now reminded them of the bad times they wanted to forget.

All she wanted to do was forget the good times with the man she'd betrayed.

James tugged the papers away from his nose. What did he mean by sniffing a stupid piece of paper? It had been nearly three weeks since he'd seen Fiona and he had no business thinking about her scent. He was trying to get her out of his mind. Besides, it only smelled of paper and ink.

And her words crept through him with a cold finality. Until now he realized he'd held out a pathetic hope that there was another side to the story. That Fiona didn't really just set out to trick him into parting with the property, that she had feelings for him, that the situation turned out differently than she expected. But her words made it clear that the scoffing journalists were entirely right. The whole scheme was planned and executed with the deft certainty of a mafia hit.

How had he been so blind? He shoved a hand through

his hair. He'd truly thought Fiona cared about him. Cold and calculating as he usually was, he'd transformed in her company and found himself craving affection and intimacy that he'd never imagined before. He'd finally grown brave enough to open his heart to a woman for the first time since that long-ago tragedy, and he'd given it to someone who was simply playing a role.

She was a very good actor.

Even now that he'd seen the evidence of her deceit written in her own hand, he had a hard time turning off the pathetic well of hope that still bubbled deep inside him. There was that one line he kept coming back to.

I was hoping my father could wait quietly for a while until we were married and happy together…

Until they were married and happy together? That sounded as if she'd actually wanted to marry him, at least by the time they rode the race. He was relieved that she hadn't been behind the media feeding frenzy and had asked her father to keep it a secret. In that one line it sounded as if she had intended to marry him, and was hoping they'd be tied together by tradition by the time he found out that he was part of a larger plan.

Would he have been as angry if in fact they did marry and he found out she'd tricked him?

He threw down the letter and paced across the great hall. The whole castle felt freezing cold and lifeless without Fiona. During her visits, she hadn't just lit a fire in the big grate, but in the entire vast building and its ponderous landscape. For the first time in as long as James could remember, the place had felt alive and fresh and full of possibilities.

If he was married to Fiona and found out that she'd come into his life only because her father had wanted that factory back…

He wouldn't have cared at all.

The realization shot through him in a jolt of electricity. All he really wanted was Fiona. With her in his life all his grand plans for acquiring and developing real estate had seemed ephemeral—entertaining but not truly important. Even his long-cultivated alliance with Beng had begun to seem like a happy side effect of the romance that swept through his life and transformed it. Once he'd decided to marry Fiona, he'd wanted to make her his wife and start their life together as soon as possible, because he was impatient and liked to get straight to the good part.

And dammit, he still wanted her.

He let out a curse, which echoed off the walls. Good thing the staff had gone to their distant quarters for the night. And another good thing that he didn't intend to drown his sorrows in whiskey like his ancestors—and then go fly a helicopter or ride out into the night.

No. He had no such reckless outlets for his pain and frustration.

He picked up a heavy glass paperweight from a table. It was probably brought back from Murano, Italy, by one of his ancestors and worth a fortune, but he didn't care. Right now he just wanted to hear something make a noise as it smashed into a million pieces.

He looked up at the carved stone crest above the fireplace, where the family's surly motto advised its members to Keep Thy Blade Sharp. He'd kept his blade honed to a vicious edge for years, and look at how much good that had done him when he was foolish enough to give his heart to a woman.

Maybe the curse was real. Maybe he was doomed to die alone and bitter, never to know the comfort of an

enduring relationship or the solace of loving someone
who loved him back.

Idiot! He should never have let himself get in so
deep. He hurled the paperweight right at the stone carving, where the metal blade shone dully amid the carved
stone. The solid glass hit with a thud, breaking loose
some stone dust, and crashed back to the floor, where it
rolled away, still in one piece. James was getting ready
to let loose another string of curses when something
else fell to the floor, too.

He glanced up. The knife blade had fallen from the
shield. No doubt that signified some kind of intensify-
ing of the curse and soon doom would rain down from
all directions. As if it wasn't already.

He glanced around the floor, but it was dark and he
couldn't see what he was looking for right away. *Who
cares?* Angus would find the blade and superglue it
back on in the morning. Since he didn't plan to climb
into a whiskey jar, maybe he could go drown himself in
stock prices on the Singapore exchange that was trading right now.

He turned to leave the room, and his foot brushed
something on the floor. He frowned and bent down to
pick it up.

"You're kidding me." His words echoed off the stone
floor as his fingers closed around the curved edge of
a tarnished metal disc. Was this it? The cup base? He
glanced up at the carved shield on the wall. A chunk
of stone was now missing beneath the inscription, and
he could make out where the disc had been wedged
into the stone carving—which in fact might well be
concrete, now that he looked closely—at just the right
angle so that only a sliver of it had been visible, as the
blade in the family crest.

The metal felt hot in his hand. At the center of the disk was a raised point, which must fit somehow into the stem of the cup. "I don't believe it."

And now he was talking to himself. The metal was incised with carvings. Rather crude workmanship, and obviously very, very old. Early medieval, possibly, or older. He remembered Katherine Drummond and her tiresome urgent messages on his phone. His life might be a shambles but at least this accursed cup could make someone happy.

He charged into the library, where her number was stored in the book, and called her. It was still a respectable hour on the East Coast of the United States.

She picked up immediately. "James, darling, how lovely to hear from you!"

"Hello, Katherine, I'm sorry it's taken me so long to get back to you. I—"

"Oh, you don't have to tell me. Your mother shared all the exciting details about your engagement to that clever girl with the decal business. I'm so happy for you."

James's heart sank. Obviously his mother hadn't been so quick to share the exciting details of his public humiliation and the revelation that his engagement was a joke on him. "Actually, it's a bit complicated, but listen…" He lifted the cup base higher, and the metal gleamed dully in the light of a nearby wall sconce. "I found the third cup piece. It was buried in the stone crest above the fireplace in the hall. It must have been there the whole time."

Katherine shrieked. "I knew it! I knew you would find it. Finally, the Drummond men will get to experience some happiness."

His chest tightened. If only this old cup had the

power to turn back the clock. But how far back would he go— to before he ever met Fiona, so he'd never know the pleasure of her company or the torture of her absence? Or just to before he left her alone at his Scottish estate—so he could see the light of curiosity flash in her eyes again or taste her lips and never know the cruel sting of betrayal. "Actually, Fiona and I aren't getting married." His voice came out flat and gruff.

"What? Your mother told me you'd be wed within the month. I've been in agonies wondering if you'd invite us or not. It's been years since I came to Scotland, and I've never seen the great Drummond estate. Did you break it off?"

"Not exactly. It's a long story."

"Oh, James. You do sound sad. Still, now that you've found the cup you can get her back and live happily ever after. It's as good as a guarantee."

"If only life really was that easy." The tarnished metal had a few dents, and it didn't look like a guarantee of anything. "Still, it does make sense to reunite the pieces of the cup and fulfill the brothers' promise to each other."

A family reunion was probably the last thing he was in the mood for right now—well, except another gossip piece in the *Straits Times*—but it had to happen so he might as well get it over with. "Why don't you talk to Jack and Sinclair and see when you can all come to Scotland. We'll have a grand ceremony here in the hall and see what kind of magic happens."

He was joking about the magic, of course.

Katherine laughed. "I'm sure lightning bolts will shoot across the skies. I can't wait! I'll see if they're free next week. Would that work for you?"

"Sure." Any week would work for him. He didn't

want to show his face in Singapore anytime soon, for obvious reasons, so he was planning to lie low here in Scotland until the fuss died down. Luckily, most people had very short memories, even for scurrilous gossip. "The hospitality of Castle Drummond awaits you at your earliest convenience." He knew she loved that kind of flourish.

He'd met Katherine several times over the years, usually on one of his mother's extravagant shopping trips to New York. He and her son, Sinclair, had both been interested in the stock market from an early age, and one time when they all stayed at a hotel down in Palm Beach. They'd spent each morning poring over stock quotes on the Telex machine in the hotel lobby, as if they were the key to all knowledge. On that same trip, or another one just like it, he'd met Jack Drummond when the latter was a rather surly teen, dragged along by his glamorous South American mother, whose command of English was surprisingly bad for someone who'd lived in the United States for more than twenty years. The reunion promised to be a diversion, at least.

"How charming! I can't wait. Well, you get on the phone with that lovely girl I heard about and patch things up so I can meet her at the reunion."

The pain of loss, edged with the cruelty of humiliation, clawed at his gut. "It's not that simple."

"It never is, but do it anyway. Now that we've found the cup you won't believe the good things that can happen."

Alone again, in the chill darkness of the empty castle that night, James found himself wishing he could call Fiona. He'd tried for three solid weeks. And the last time he tried, someone called Julio had answered and said he had the wrong number, so she'd apparently changed her phone number to avoid him. His emails bounced back unread, each feeling like a hard slap to his face. He should hate her, but he didn't even have that satisfaction.

Because he missed her too much.

He went to bed feeling as cold and grim as the old stone walls. Even the prospect of all the beautiful women whom he'd never met held no appeal. The idea of jumping back on the dating merry-go-round and making small talk to girls he had nothing in common with only made him long for Fiona's sharp insight and unexpected affections.

He couldn't phone her. He couldn't email her. So the one option left was to track her down in person.

Eleven

Fiona's address was written on the back of her envelope. 1732 Whitefern Road, San Diego, California. He didn't know if it was her house, or her parents', or if she was staying with a friend. It didn't really matter.

His pilot flew him into San Diego International Airport. He'd arranged a rented car but had to wait a frustrating twenty minutes while they prepared it. He entered Fiona's address into his GPS and set out into the darkening streets of the unfamiliar city, adrenaline pounding in his blood.

It was nearly 9:00 p.m. by the time he pulled onto leafy Whitefern Road and found himself peering through the darkness for house numbers.

His pulse thudded dully, but his brain was on high alert. He didn't know what he intended to say to Fiona, but he did know he couldn't just let her walk away after everything that had happened between them.

The number *1732* flashed at him from a mailbox, so he pulled into the driveway and killed the engine. A light flickered in the window, suggesting a television on somewhere. He climbed out and shut the car door quietly, wanting to keep surprise on his side in case she decided to hide from him once again.

He held his breath as the doorbell chimed. *Who could that be?* A distant voice. Not Fiona's. *I'll get it.*

He heard footsteps moving closer and he braced himself as the door handle turned. A tall, striking woman with long braided hair answered. She stood expectantly in the doorway, as if waiting for him to announce his purpose.

"I'm looking for Fiona Lam."

"Really." She arched a brow. "And you are?"

"James Drummond."

"I knew it." She pulled the door open and gestured for him to enter.

For some reason, that wasn't the response he expected, so he stood for a moment before entering. "Fiona, darling, it's for you," she called.

"I didn't order anything. I thought we were going out."

Her voice, from a distant room, made his pulse pound in his temples. An urge to rush forward seized him, and it took every ounce of strength to keep his cool.

"It's a *visitor* for you." Her tall friend eyed him from head to toe with obvious amusement. "I understand things a lot better now that I've seen you in the flesh," she whispered. She extended her hand and he shook it. "I'm Crystal."

A hush descended as Fiona rounded a corner and stopped dead. Even the distant TV sizzled into white noise as adrenaline surged through him. "Hello, Fiona."

* * *

Fiona realized she'd finally gone mad and started seeing visions. Not Banquo's ghost, but James Drummond, larger than life and standing in Crystal's living room.

"Aren't you even going to say hello?" Crystal's voice jolted her from a fog of confusion.

"James?" She didn't trust her eyes. Or any other part of her. Her heart raced and she fought a violent urge to run into his arms, which were not exactly stretched out to welcome her.

"Can we talk alone?" His tone was serious.

"And have me miss all the fun?" Crystal teased. "All right. I'll go hide in the bedroom in my own house so you two can straighten out the mess you made." She turned and headed up the stairs. Fiona wanted to beg her to stay. *Don't leave me alone with him.* But wasn't this what she'd secretly hoped for when she printed her address so carefully on the back of the envelope?

"I'm so sorry." The words rushed out of her on a wave of relief that she could finally say them to his face. "I know I should never have done it. I didn't think it through and things got out of control, and I…"

He stepped forward and silenced her with his mouth. His kiss was fierce, almost cruel, and she yielded to it instantly, clutching him close and kissing him back with every ounce of strength she had left.

His lips pulled away, leaving her shaking. "Don't think I've forgiven you." His eyes were narrowed, dark slate-gray and unreadable. "I haven't."

She swallowed. Now desire pulsed through her like a stray cat loose in the house. Her thoughts tangled and tumbled over each other. "I haven't forgiven myself, either. I should have told you the truth—about my father and the factory—but it all moved so fast and there was never a right time, and then it was too late."

"You made a fool of me. Not just in the press, but in the privacy of my own home."

She shivered. "Everything that happened between us... None of that was pretend. I really meant it."

"How could you say that when all along you were playing me over a piece of property?"

"I started out wanting the property, to make my father happy, but as I got to know you, I...I..." *Why not?* "I fell in love with you." The words tripped over each other and came out jumbled.

"You have a strange way of showing it." Humor glittered darkly in his eyes, along with something more intense.

"It wasn't fair of you to ask me to marry you when I barely knew you."

"You could have said no." He cocked his head.

"Did you think I would?"

"No." His egotism was infuriating.

"See? Maybe the whole thing was a self-fulfilling prophecy. You thought I'd marry you just because you were handsome and rich and had a castle. Is that a good way to entice your life partner? You should get to know someone and find out what makes them tick before you try to take them down the aisle."

That glint of humor in his eyes had a hard edge. "I admit my own aims were somewhat mercenary. I needed a wife so I could look respectable to my Singapore business contacts. That rather backfired."

"I heard." She spoke softly. "Though maybe you had it coming. You shouldn't marry for any reason except love."

"You really are insufferably arrogant." He stood taller, and seemed to tower over her.

"Look who's talking! You're so used to running your own show you have no idea what to do when someone else has a different agenda."

"Normally, I find a way to change their mind."

"Well, you can't always have your own way." She pulled herself up as tall as she could, which wasn't very tall, especially in flip-flops. And she became painfully aware that she was wearing flannel pajama bottoms and a T-shirt with a duck on it.

"Not with you around." His eyes narrowed. "And dammit, I do want you around." He stepped close again but instead of zeroing in for the kill this time, he let his mouth hover just over hers, as if testing her to see if she could manage not to kiss him.

She couldn't. Their lips met, hot and wet, and her fingers thrust into his hair as she tugged him close. She felt his hands roaming up and down her back, pressing into her, almost lifting her off the ground with the force of his embrace.

It was so good to hold him again, to let herself fall into his arms and lose herself in his heated kisses. "You're coming with me." He breathed the words into her ear.

"Where to?" His hotel?

"Scotland."

"But I have a meeting tomorrow with—"

"Cancel it."

"Okay." Proctor & Gamble could wait. "Am I allowed to pack?"

"I'll watch while you pack. I'm not taking my eyes off you for an instant. I have no idea what you'll do next."

His gray eyes bored a hole into her while she shoved

some clothes into a duffel bag and tried to hide her fist-
fuls of lingerie inside a plain gray T-shirt.

"I need to change." Was she supposed to strip down
right in front of him? Even though he'd seen it all before, it felt weird.

"Nonsense. I like ducks. Let's go." His face had an
intensity she'd never seen before. This whole thing was
weird, like a crazy dream—or nightmare—and she had
no idea what was going to happen next, but she knew
she had to go with him.

His private jet flew them to somewhere on the east
coast of Canada for refueling, then on to Scotland. She
kept expecting to hear some kind of explanation of what
he planned, but none was offered. James was very busy
on his laptop for much of the time, with only a murmured explanation that a big market move was under-
way and he had to pay close attention.

She didn't even want to argue or demand more details. Sitting here quietly in her pj's while the plane
hummed through the night sky felt like the beginning
of a rigorous and entirely deserved punishment for her
sins.

It was daylight by the time they landed in Aberdeen
and James's driver put their bags in the trunk. "That
was a quick trip, sir."

James murmured a gruff assent. As he climbed into
the back next to her, he whispered in her ear, "I feel
like a repo man."

His breath, hot on her skin, stirred the emotion she'd
tried so hard to keep under control. "Demanding pay-
ment of debts?" She couldn't even remember what repo
men did.

"Taking back what was mine all along." His mouth

met hers again in a hot kiss that made her skin prickle with awareness. As the car pulled away with them in the backseat, he deepened the kiss, wrapping his arms around her and holding her tight against his chest.

When he was done he sat very still, staring out the window. She still had no idea what to say, so she didn't say anything.

Her heart swelled with a mix of fear and anticipation as they followed the road along the berm that edged the estate and then turned into the long drive. She'd been so sure she'd never see this beautiful place again.

Pale morning sun bathed the landscape, heightening the colors and making it seem even more like a fairy-tale kingdom. When the car pulled up in front of the castle, the driver opened her door and she set her first flip-flop onto the gravel, feeling the sudden chill of the air. Smoke from a fire and the rich smell of damp earth filled her nostrils. It was ridiculous how much she'd missed this place.

James took her arm, an interesting formal touch, and they walked up the front steps. "You're in your usual room," was all he said before he disappeared.

Alone in her room, with her bag brought by one of the staff, she immediately checked the top drawer of the dresser, where she'd left the ring. Still there, twinkling quietly against the dark wood.

Her stomach tightened. Did he not see the note at the bottom of her letter? This ring must be worth a fortune. Even a wealthy man like James couldn't simply forget about it.

Or did he intend for her to put it back on? Heart pounding, she pulled it from the drawer and slipped it back onto her finger. It fit snugly and glittered ostentatiously against her skin.

No. Too presumptuous. She took it back off and placed it carefully in the drawer. She even found herself glancing over her shoulder as she slid the drawer closed. She was embarrassed by the idea that someone might see her revisiting the recent—yet so distant—past when she had been James's intended fiancée.

She showered and changed into a simple black dress with a row of buttons down the front. As she did them up she wondered if James's fingers would be next to touch the tiny mother-of-pearl buttons. Her belly shivered at the idea, but she tried to push it from her mind. No sense jumping to conclusions.

She knew that dinner was served at eight, so she came down only one minute early, not wanting to find herself alone in the grand rooms, looking awkwardly at the paintings and smiling politely at the staff, while James was nowhere to be seen.

The smell of roast meat filled the dining room already, and she almost jumped when she saw James, also dressed in black, at the far end of the room. "I asked the staff to leave dinner for us. We're on our own."

She wasn't sure whether to be relieved or scared. What punishment had James in mind when he bundled her into his private jet and brought her here? The hard planes of his face offered no clues. "Let's eat."

They helped themselves to racks of lamb, roast potatoes and delicate baby carrots, and sat at the polished wood table—large enough to seat forty—in a silence that grew more deafening with each passing second.

Three glasses each glittered with a different color of wine, but she didn't dare take a sip as she didn't want her judgment any more clouded than it already was. She managed a few bites of the delicious food, but finally she couldn't stand the oppressive quiet anymore.

"Do you intend to run me though and hang me from the battlements?"

James stared at her for a moment, then threw back his head and laughed. "Tempting as that might seem, I don't want to compound my social disgrace by becoming a murderer."

"Understandable. Perhaps it would be more convenient if I ran myself through."

"No doubt, but please don't." A light shimmered in his eyes. Otherwise, his face was hard as granite. "I have a more fitting punishment in mind."

"What's that?" She never did like suspense.

"I think you should be forced to follow through on the promises you made." His gray eyes regarded her steadily. "I held up my end of our bargains."

Her heart beat faster and she mustered all her strength to keep a poker face. "True." Did he mean that he still wanted to marry her? And if so, was it only to make the rest of her life a living hell? "What exactly did you have in mind?"

"Marriage, of course."

She battled the rush of excitement that threatened to derail all common sense. "Why would you want to marry someone you can't trust?"

His eyes narrowed, until they looked almost black. "Keep your enemies close."

"Another school of thought holds that it makes more sense to move to a different continent and forget all about them."

His eyes glittered with amusement. "I think the Drummonds would regard that as cowardice."

"Ouch. You probably shouldn't marry a coward, either."

"Oh, you're no coward. Just cautious. You knew

it was a good idea to put distance between us until I cooled off." He leaned back in his chair. "Very sensible, under the circumstances."

She swallowed. "So…you're asking me to marry you?"

"Oh, no." His swift answer made her stomach clench. "I already did that. I don't like to repeat myself. Especially when the results weren't impressive the first time."

She blinked. He was toying with her. "You think I should decide whether to follow through on my promises."

He watched her coolly. "I think you already did, by coming here."

"I didn't have much choice." Her blood was pounding in her head. Did she really have a chance to do this over?

"You always have a choice."

Inscrutable as a pharaoh, he sat and watched her from across the gleaming expanse of polished wood. She wanted to throw food at him, or run and kiss him, or scream and run around. Anything but sit here as if she was in a board meeting with a cold-eyed boss.

James Drummond wanted to marry her, even after all she'd done. But there was no affection here, no promises of a happy life together. No declarations of love.

"You don't love me." The words sounded plaintive, almost pathetic, on her tongue. It wouldn't hurt if only she hadn't fallen so foolishly in love with him.

"Dammit, Fiona!" He smashed his fist on the table, which made her jump a foot in the air. His chair fell back as he rose to his feet. "I love you so much I can barely breathe." He strode around the table. "I love you so much I can't get out of bed in the morning without aching for the sight of you." He pulled her roughly up from her chair. "I love you so much I can't bear the thought of living without you."

He held her hands tight, and for the first time she could read the emotion in the stormy depth of his eyes. Every muscle in his body was tight, a coiled spring ready to explode with unexpressed emotion. "I love you so much I don't know what the hell I'll do if you don't marry me."

Her only response was a throaty sob that exploded from her without permission. She jumped into his arms and hugged him. "I love you, too, James." Now her voice really sounded pathetic. "I've missed you every second. I didn't think I'd ever see you again, and it was killing me. I've never met anyone like you, and it didn't take me long to figure out that you and I are almost ridiculously perfect for each other. It hurt so badly when I realized I'd ruined everything."

His arms around her felt so good. Emotion crashed through her in waves, and she kept having to look into his eyes to make sure this was really happening.

"I'll take my share of the blame, too." He spoke gruffly. "I didn't listen when you wanted to slow down. That didn't fit my needs, and they were all I worried about. I was an ass."

"We were both asses." She bit her lip. "I guess that's why we tycoons aren't often popular."

He laughed and hugged her close. "We'd drive anyone crazy, except each other."

"And maybe even each other, too. I do love you, James. I love you very, very much."

This time their kiss was soft and tender. And led to a night of lovemaking that confirmed what they both already knew—they were meant to be together.

Epilogue

"Don't worry, it won't rain." Katherine Drummond beamed at the slate-gray skies over the sweeping lawn behind James's castle. "Not now that we've found the cup." Katherine had been at James Drummond's magnificent estate for only one night, but already she felt more a Drummond than ever. The entire estate was in celebration mode. Staff dashed around making final preparations for the wedding, and guests had been arriving all morning from far and wide.

"When are you going to put the cup together?" Annie asked. Sinclair's wife had been there—as his housekeeper—when Katherine first came up with the idea to find the pieces.

"When Jack arrives. Even though we have his piece with us, it won't be the same unless he's here." She glanced at her watch. Nearly 11:25 a.m. and Fiona and James's wedding was at noon sharp. "I hope he hurries up. It would be terrible if he missed the wedding. And I'm sure it would bring good luck to have the cup reunited at the ceremony."

"Sinclair and I have survived several months of marriage with the cup in pieces." Annie smiled. "So it's not a big deal if they have to wait."

Katherine smoothed the silky skirt of her dress. "I know. It's just that we've waited so long already. I thought James would never bother to find his piece. In fact, none of you were very helpful." She poked her son in the ribs. "Sinclair didn't seem to care at all about the cup. But you'll thank me for it a few decades from now when you're still happily married." She instinctively glanced at her watch again: 11:26. "Where is Jack? Is he sailing here from Florida on one of his boats?"

"Don't worry, Aunt Katherine." James, tall and handsome as ever, kissed her on the cheek. "I just got a text that he's minutes away. The fate of the Drummonds is in good hands."

"Where's your blushing bride?" she teased. Fiona did not seem like the blushing type. In fact, she seemed steely enough to manage any Drummond, even one with a large castle.

"I'm not allowed to see her in her wedding finery until she comes down the aisle. You know how we feel about traditions here in Scotland."

"And you know how much I love that! I should have worn the family tartan. How come you're not in a kilt, James?"

"Kilts are a trifling nineteenth-century fashion. We Drummonds are a far more ancient race and prefer to keep our knees covered."

"Quite understandable, though I'm sure you have a fine set of knees." She sighed. The Drummond men were so handsome it was no wonder they had women falling all over them throughout the centuries. Once the cup was reunited, they'd finally be able to enjoy the kind of happy marriage she'd hoped for when she'd married her own dashing Drummond nearly forty years ago. She hadn't been able to save him from his demons, but she'd be damned if she was going to see the next generation succumb to some old curse.

The throaty purr of an expensive engine made heads turn, and she smiled when she saw the always elegant Vicki climb out from the passenger side of a low-slung sports car. An old family friend, Vicki was the perfect match for Jack Drummond, descendant of the piratical branch of the family.

"Darling." Katherine kissed Vicki on both cheeks when she approached the group. "Thank you for corralling your husband here. I'm sure it wasn't easy."

Jack managed to look rather wild and untamed even in a sleek suit. "So you're going to set us all on the straight and narrow." He hugged her. "I'm not sure I'm ready for that, but I'll do my best."

"Oh, I don't think it will be at all narrow. And probably not too straight, either. But now that everyone's here we can finally put the cup back together after three hundred years."

"But we haven't even tested the pieces to see if they fit yet." Annie was definitely a worrier like herself. Which was good when you had a Drummond at home, though Sinclair was hardly wild. It was wonderful to see them so happy, and she was eagerly anticipating the new Drummond who'd soon be running around their old Long Island house.

"They'll fit. We wise old ladies know these things." She tried to smile inscrutably.

"Old?" Vicki laughed. "You look younger than all of us. I want your plastic surgeon's number."

"I won't have anything to do with surgery. I rely entirely on miracles. Speaking of which, let's gather the pieces of the cup and get ready."

Fiona's heart swelled with emotion as she walked down the aisle, arm in arm with James, after their sweet and simple ceremony had joined them together as husband and wife. The aisle was simply a broad strip of grass between two phalanxes of chairs filled with glamorous wedding guests, including James's mom, her own mom and stepdad, and—gasp!—her dad. James had invited him to dine with them in Singapore, anxious to meet the man who'd inspired such creative conspiring against him. He and her dad hit it off, and the meal had ended with them brainstorming ways to bring her dad's business into the twenty-first century. They'd since spent time together here in Scotland, and their unconventional family was evolving beyond her expectations.

The three pieces of the cup lay on a tartan draped over a table at the far end of the aisle. The three Drummond men, James, Jack and Sinclair, would each take a piece and join them again, as their ancestors had intended when the cup was last split three hundred years ago.

James took the base that had flung itself at him from the wall of his own castle. Jack took the drinking vessel that he'd dredged up from under the sea near his island in Florida, and Sinclair took the stem that had lain quietly amid the accumulated clutter in the attic of his Long Island mansion.

Fiona held her breath as James held the base steady,

and Sinclair pushed the stem down onto a raised point in the middle. It slid neatly into place. Jack lifted the bowl and held it over the stem, then lowered it slowly until the two pieces slid together to form an apparently seamless chalice.

"Oh, my goodness," Katherine said, clearly overwhelmed with emotion. "Look, it fits! I always knew the legend was true. Where's the champagne?"

The skies had brightened and tiny white clouds scudded across pale blue. Birds darted around as a waiter filled the chalice with champagne and the Drummonds and their new brides passed it around, drinking to the future generations.

Annie only pretended to sip as she was several months pregnant with their first baby. The expectant mother glowed with happiness. But apparently that wasn't enough for Katherine. "So, who's going to produce the next member of the new generation?"

"Don't look at me just yet." Fiona hugged James. They'd decided to launch a new business together in Singapore, and they would be busy flying back and forth for at least the next year. Maybe then they'd settle in Scotland and throw themselves into domesticity.

Jack elbowed his wife. The usually pale Vicki blushed an uncharacteristic beetroot. "I'm in the market for designer maternity wear. Apparently the next Drummond is a male and will be arriving in only six months' time."

Katherine gasped and looked as if she might faint, then burst into hysterical laughter. "Perfect! I'm so happy I could cry. In fact, I think it's a very strong possibility."

"Congratulations, Vicki." Fiona hugged her new cousin. "And congratulations, Annie," she added, kissing Annie's soft cheek. "I can't wait to be the favorite aunt for the youngest Drummonds. You'll have to bring them here often so they can get in touch with their Scottish heritage."

"And learn to hunt," chimed in James.

"It's obvious the Drummonds will never be entirely tamed, but I suppose that's a good thing." Katherine patted her eye makeup carefully with a tissue. "Now, let's dance!"

* * * * *

COMING NEXT MONTH from Harlequin Desire®
AVAILABLE APRIL 2, 2013

#2221 PLAYING FOR KEEPS
The Alpha Brotherhood
Catherine Mann

Malcolm Douglas uses his secret Interpol connections to protect his childhood sweetheart when her life is in danger. But their close proximity reignites flames they thought were long burned out.

#2222 NO STRANGER TO SCANDAL
Daughters of Power: The Capital
Rachel Bailey

Will a young reporter struggling to prove herself fall for the older single dad who's investigating her family's news network empire—with the intention of destroying it?

#2223 IN THE RANCHER'S ARMS
Rich, Rugged Ranchers
Kathie DeNosky

A socialite running from her father's scandals answers an ad for a mail-order bride. But when she falls for the wealthy rancher, she worries the truth will come out.

#2224 MILLIONAIRE IN A STETSON
Colorado Cattle Barons
Barbara Dunlop

The missing diary of heiress Niki Gerard's mother triggers an all-out scandal. While she figures out who she can trust, the new rancher in town stirs up passions...and harbors secrets of his own.

#2225 PROJECT: RUNAWAY HEIRESS
Project: Passion
Heidi Betts

A fashionista goes undercover to find out who's stealing her company's secrets but can't resist sleeping with the enemy when it comes to her new British billionaire boss.

#2226 CAROSELLI'S BABY CHASE
The Caroselli Inheritance
Michelle Celmer

The marketing specialist brought in to shake up Robert Caroselli's workaday world is the same woman he had a New Year's one-night stand with—and she's pregnant with his baby!

You can find more information on upcoming Harlequin® titles, free excerpts and more at www.Harlequin.com.

HDCNM0313

REQUEST YOUR FREE BOOKS!
2 FREE NOVELS PLUS 2 FREE GIFTS!

HARLEQUIN® *Desire*

ALWAYS POWERFUL, PASSIONATE AND PROVOCATIVE

YES! Please send me 2 FREE Harlequin Desire® novels and my 2 FREE gifts (gifts are worth about $10). After receiving them, if I don't wish to receive any more books, I can return the shipping statement marked "cancel." If I don't cancel, I will receive 6 brand-new novels every month and be billed just $4.30 per book in the U.S. or $4.99 per book in Canada. That's a savings of at least 14% off the cover price! It's quite a bargain! Shipping and handling is just 50¢ per book in the U.S. and 75¢ per book in Canada.* I understand that accepting the 2 free books and gifts places me under no obligation to buy anything. I can always return a shipment and cancel at any time. Even if I never buy another book, the two free books and gifts are mine to keep forever.

225/326 HDN FVP7

Name _____ (PLEASE PRINT)

Address _____ Apt. #

City _____ State/Prov. _____ Zip/Postal Code

Signature (if under 18, a parent or guardian must sign)

Mail to the **Harlequin**® **Reader Service:**
IN U.S.A.: P.O. Box 1867, Buffalo, NY 14240-1867
IN CANADA: P.O. Box 609, Fort Erie, Ontario L2A 5X3

Want to try two free books from another line?
Call 1-800-873-8635 or visit www.ReaderService.com.

* Terms and prices subject to change without notice. Prices do not include applicable taxes. Sales tax applicable in N.Y. Canadian residents will be charged applicable taxes. Offer not valid in Quebec. This offer is limited to one order per household. Not valid for current subscribers to Harlequin Desire books. All orders subject to credit approval. Credit or debit balances in a customer's account(s) may be offset by any other outstanding balance owed by or to the customer. Please allow 4 to 6 weeks for delivery. Offer available while quantities last.

Your Privacy—The Harlequin® Reader Service is committed to protecting your privacy. Our Privacy Policy is available online at www.ReaderService.com or upon request from the Harlequin Reader Service.

We make a portion of our mailing list available to reputable third parties that offer products we believe may interest you. If you prefer that we not exchange your name with third parties, or if you wish to clarify or modify your communication preferences, please visit us at www.ReaderService.com/consumerschoice or write to us at Harlequin Reader Service Preference Service, P.O. Box 9062, Buffalo, NY 14269. Include your complete name and address.

HDI3

Midway through the junior high choir's rehearsal of "It's a Small World," Celia Patel found out just how small the world could shrink.

She dodged as half the singers—the female half—sprinted down the stands, squealing in fan-girl glee. All their preteen energy was focused on racing to where he stood.

Malcolm Douglas.

Seven-time Grammy Award winner.

Platinum-selling soft rock star.

And the man who'd broken Celia's heart when they were both sixteen years old.

Malcolm raised a stalling hand to his ominous body-guards while keeping his eyes locked on Celia, smiling that million-watt grin. Tall and honed, he still had a hometown-boy-handsome appeal. He'd merely matured—now polished with confidence and whipcord muscle.

She wanted him gone.

For her sanity's sake, she *needed* him gone. But now that he was here, she couldn't look away.

He wore his khakis and Ferragamo loafers with the easy confidence of a man comfortable in his skin. Sleeves rolled up on his chambray shirt exposed strong, tanned forearms and musician's hands.

Best not to think about his talented, nimble hands.

His sandy-brown hair was as thick as she remembered. It was still a little long, skimming over his forehead in a way that once called to her fingers to stroke it back. And those blue eyes—heaven help her…

There was no denying, he was all man now.

What in the hell was he doing here?

Malcolm hadn't set foot in Azalea, Mississippi, since a judge crony of her father's had offered Malcolm the choice of juvie or military reform school nearly eighteen years ago. Since he'd left her behind—scared, *pregnant* and determined to salvage her life.

But they weren't sixteen anymore, and she'd put aside reckless dreams the day she'd handed her newborn daughter over to a couple who could give the precious child everything Celia and Malcolm couldn't.

She threw back her shoulders and started across the gym.

She refused to let Malcolm's appearance yank the rug out from under her blessedly routine existence. She refused to give him the power to send her pulse racing.

She refused to let Malcolm Douglas threaten the future she'd built for herself.

What is Malcolm doing back in town?

Find out in

PLAYING FOR KEEPS

Available April 2013 from Harlequin® Desire!